I0520898

Kensei

Jeremy Zimmerman

Copyright © 2012 Jeremy Zimmerman

All rights reserved.

Originally published as part of *Cobalt City Rookies* by Timid Pirate
Publishing.

Cover illustration and layout by Katie Nyborg.

ISBN: 0615905951
ISBN-13:978- 0615905952

DEDICATION

This book is dedicated to my lovely wife, Dawn, who has stood by my side when she hasn't been kicking me to write.

CONTENTS

	Acknowledgments	i
Chapter 1	A Night on the Town	1
Chapter 2	Boys and Girls	8
Chapter 3	Home Life	16
Chapter 4	Back on the Street	26
Chapter 5	2thefairest	33
Chapter 6	Major Tomboy	43
Chapter 7	In Crowd and Out Crowd	51
Chapter 8	More Bloodsucking Owls	59
Chapter 9	More Apples	67
Chapter 10	Kids These Days	77
Chapter 11	New Things Come to Light	83
Chapter 12	Working for the Weekend	91
Chapter 13	Sudden But Inevitable Betrayal	100
Chapter 14	We Need a Bigger Boat	105
Chapter 15	Legacies	119
Chapter 16	Keeping Secrets	132
Chapter 17	Awkward Conversations	149
Chapter 18	To Catch a God	154
Chapter 19	Gods and Monsters	162
Chapter 20	Fade to Black	174

ACKNOWLEDGMENTS

All things arise from conditions, and this book is no different. Many people have helped me to beat this book into shape, and they deserve a hearty hurrah. Folly Blaine, Andrew Cherry, Melissa Dominic, Jamie Lackey, Chloë Liotta-Jones, Nayad Monroe, Kath Nyborg, Jenna Pitman, Torrey Podmajersky, Lauren Scanlan, David Vandenabeele, Catherine Warren, and Chris Ybarra all read through different phases of the book and offered invaluable assistance in beating it into shape. Jennifer Gilpin, Wayne Saito, and Keala Jordan were all invaluable Subject Matter Experts in their own particular idioms. Caren Gussoff gave me much needed encouragement and resources on writing someone very different from myself. Jet City Roller Girls and Seattle Derby Brats both provided many opportunities to learn more about the nuts and bolts of roller derby both as a sport and a culture. In particular I'd like to thank Betty Ford Galaxy, Connie Torturous, Hockey Honey, and Katy Didit for fielding random questions, especially when I didn't always know what I wanted to know (and sometimes didn't follow up with). Ian Ng, Stiletto Libretto, Heidi Your Boyfriend, and my wife (in her role as Vladi Impaler) helped me create Cobalt City's Goblin Town Roller Girls. Rev. Don Castro of Seattle Buddhist Church was patient and helpful in assisting me in better understanding Jodo Shinshu Buddhism. Nathan Crowder deserves any praise or blame for looking at a short story and asking me for more. And, more than anything, none of this would have been possible without my wife, Dawn Vogel.

i

CHAPTER 1 - A NIGHT ON THE TOWN

Kensei crouched at the corner of the rooftop and peered below. A few pedestrians walked past, but the streets were mostly empty. Even the usual wannabes were missing from the front of Tobacco Mart. A chill autumn wind rose off of the Puckwudgie River and crept through every possible gap in her *shinobi shozoku* and the sweat-soaked thermal underwear she wore underneath.

A sense of vertigo hit, reminding her of how little sleep she'd gotten the last couple nights. She'd hoped to take tonight off, catch up on homework and get to bed early. But the spirit of the neighborhood had warned her something bad was coming and, as much as she hated to admit it, he was usually right. The only sign of villainy she'd found, though, was the cracking, slurred voice of a drunk man singing karaoke in Kosta's Sports Bar and Greek Grill. And that was only a crime against music. Even the spirits of the darkest alleys seemed relaxed, as if no violence would mar their domains.

Chatter streamed through her left earbud from the police scanner. Superheroes Huntsman and Libertine had apprehended a mugger in Quayside. Something eight feet tall and hairy had just broken into Cobalt City First National Bank downtown, and cops yelled back and forth about what to do. As if in response, Kensei saw a golden streak of light shoot from Starcom Tower. Jaccob Stevens, tech mogul and publicly known as the superhero Stardust, must be responding. At least a few other superheroes were out on the street.

1

"Go get 'em, Stardust," Kensei whispered to the distant superhero.

She wished more heroes still called Cobalt City their home, but things had gotten bad the last several years. If the bank wasn't on the other side of town, she might have gone to help. But she still hadn't taken the time to practice driving, which meant no license for her. And there was the whole threat to the neighborhood. But it was tempting to have something actually happen.

"This is very bad, Miss Hattori," said a familiar male voice behind her, referring to her by her birth name.

"Jeez, Karl," she said through gritted teeth, her heart pounding in her chest. "When are you going to stop trying to scare the crap out of me?"

She turned and looked back at the spirit, who seemed oblivious to her comment, staring off into the night. Kensei had one superpower: the ability to see and talk with spirits of places and things like Karl. Though he appeared to stand next to her, it was clear he wasn't a physical thing. Instead, he stood superimposed in her line of vision, like a smudge on a pair of sunglasses. If she wasn't so sure she was the only one around who could see or hear him, she might object to being referred to by her real name. But Karl was old-fashioned and did not care much for assumed names.

"I think you're worrying about nothing," Kensei said. "All the bad guys must be taking the night off. Even the O'Reillys are taking a break from screaming at each other."

Karl shook his head. "No, there is badness here. I feel it in my gut. Something tearing and biting inside."

Karlsburg was a neighborhood of immigrants, and Karl was the manifestation of that neighborhood. He almost always looked male with gray hair and a thick moustache, dressed in a suit that was probably fashionable fifty years ago in the old country. Otherwise, his appearance could have belonged to any of dozens of distant countries. Some days he looked Greek, other days Russian, and sometimes Ethiopian. Kensei always felt weird when he used a non-human shape. Apparently, not all the immigrants in Karlsburg came from this planet.

"And you're sure it isn't something you ate?" Kensei said with a sigh.

"I told you before, I don't eat."

"I know. That was a joke. Again." Kensei scratched at an itch between her dreadlocks under the *tenugui* she had wrapped around her head for a mask. Her usual banter with the spirit felt forced and meaner than usual. She chalked it up to exhaustion. "But this little superhero is half asleep, failing algebra and this is a school night. If something doesn't happen soon, I'll need to go to bed and hope that some other masked avenger is around to bust it up."

"This is nothing to joke about," Karl said.

"I'm not joking," Kensei said. "If looks could kill, I would have been a dead girl when my mom saw my progress report. My dad is cool with the superheroics, but Mom doesn't know about it at all. And she can't know. Dad can only run interference for so long before she insists on me finishing my senior year in a boarding school. And then you'll need to look for someone else to help out. Seriously, Stardust is in the freaking phone book. I can leave a message at Starcom's reception desk and then go to bed."

"You are the protector of this neighborhood," Karl growled. "You have a duty—"

"You know how my mom feels about super-heroes! It's hard to maintain my lie when I'm spending all night running around with a stolen katana and dressed like a ninja!"

"Hey!" a man's voice yelled from a nearby apartment building. "Shut up and go back to your padded cell at Fermi!"

Kensei froze, not realizing she'd been yelling.

"If not you, who?" Karl asked, ignoring the other voice.

"And if not now, when?" she said. As exhausted as she felt, she thought she might cry soon. "Thanks, John F. Kennedy. I've traveled this guilt trip before."

"You finally found out who said that?" Karl asked. "How many years—"

A woman's scream cut off anything further from Karl. Kensei turned and ran in the direction of the sound, ignoring the "I told you so" that Karl called out after her.

"No, please, no!" the woman yelled out.

A man replied, "Just let go of the purse, lady, and this'll be over much faster."

Kensei came to the edge of a roof above an alley and looked down twenty feet to see a young man struggling to take a purse from a woman curled up in a ball. He kicked her and she screamed and sobbed. The young hero backed up a few steps before running and leaping off the roof. As she dropped, she angled herself to hit the mugger with both feet.

And then she hit concrete and stumbled with the unexpected impact. She had passed through the mugger as though he wasn't there. When her footing was stable, she drew her katana and turned to face the mugger, but the alley was empty. No mugger, no woman. Just wet and moldering trash at the edges. Something seemed off about the alley, though she couldn't place what it was. A yellow apple with something carved into the side sat where the mugging had been. She walked toward it, wincing at the pain in her right ankle, and bent down to pick it up.

Up close, she could make out that someone had cut Greek letters into the side of the apple: καλλίστῃ. She focused on the apple, trying to examine its spiritual energy, and nearly dropped it. Normally she only saw more aware spirits, but with effort she could see the small spirits of individual objects and see traces of magic. In this case, the spirit of the apple looked like a round mass of writhing black worms, the letters shining with golden light.

The sound of footsteps drew Kensei's attention away from the apple. At both ends of the alley, dozens of armed men and women walked towards her. There was no way they could have been there a second ago, but now they filled the alley in either direction. They ranged in age and ethnicity, and many of them looked like the sort of criminals that normally hung out in Karlsburg. She even spotted Mr. and Mrs. O'Reilly. Apparently every jerk, creep, and criminal in the area had decided to ambush her.

Hooray for community? She didn't even think all these people knew her.

"I'm open for suggestions on how to get out of here, Karl," Kensei whispered. She glanced around and didn't see the spirit anywhere. Or, really, any spirit. The alley's spirit, a small starving child, was nowhere to be seen. The spirits of the buildings, normally curious about any possible threats to their domain, were notably absent. A cold dread settled into her gut. "Karl?"

That's when it hit her. The strange sensation she had experienced before was the absence of these spirits. She could still feel some spiritual energy. She could faintly feel the spirits of the winds drifting past her, but everything else around her had become muffled and distant.

The spirit of her katana, in an uncharacteristically talkative moment, growled, "*baka*," the Japanese word for idiot.

As the mob advanced, Kensei gave up on Karl. She tried to think of some great wisdom from Musashi's *The Book of Five Rings* but all she could think was, "Oh crap."

She dropped the apple and ran towards one group, parrying a blow from a baseball bat with her sword, and punched the large man holding it in the face. He staggered back, silent and non-reactive to his broken and bloody nose. Kensei's fear of the situation moved up another notch.

She sheathed her katana and climbed up one of the members of the mob to grab hold of the fire escape ladder. Clumsy blows from clubs left her legs stinging. She even felt a knife rake along her shin before she pulled herself up and out of the way. She was glad she had gotten her tetanus shot not too long ago.

Blood ran down her leg as she climbed up the ladder. As she neared the top, she glanced back down to see the mob trying to climb up after her. She turned her attention back towards the roof and saw a few dozen more people coming at her along the rooftop. Kensei fought down the urge to cry as things went from bad to worse.

"This is going to suck," she said.

~

Kensei limped up to a brick wall in a blind alley and leaned against it, catching her breath. Her body felt like she'd gone a few rounds with a meat tenderizer.

"Karl? Am I clear?" she asked. Normally the spirit of the neighborhood played lookout for her, but since the ambush he'd been missing. Out of the alley, the deadened spiritual energy had diminished, but it still lingered in the air half a mile away.

When Karl didn't answer, she cursed and turned to make a token effort to spot anyone watching her. Then she whispered to the wall, "The devil, you say." The wall in front of her rotated with a portion of the pavement in front of it as it turned to face the interior of the building. A light came on automatically and she walked over to enter in a code onto an ancient keypad next to a metal door. The door slid open and she stumbled into her secret lair, tearing off her sweat-soaked mask and symbolically shifting out of her role as Kensei and into her role as Jamie Hattori.

She collapsed onto the foam rubber mat tucked into the corner.

She lay there with a groan of pain, relishing the experience of not moving. She ached, and she knew her body would be one big bruise in the morning.

"There you are!" Karl appeared next to her heavy punching bag. "I lost track of you. What happened?"

"I was going to ask you that," Jamie mumbled into the foam rubber. "The mugging turned into a big ambush."

"That... that isn't possible," Karl said. "I would know if there was to be an ambush."

"And yet it happened. And now I hurt. A lot. It felt like something had muffled the spirits in the area. Might be a side effect." Jamie lifted her head, reached inside her costume and pulled out her cell phone to look at the clock. When she saw the time, she dropped her head back onto the foam rubber. "Crap. I need to get home and get to bed."

"You could have died, Miss Hattori. And I had no idea it was to happen. How can you think of bed at a time like this?"

Jamie stumbled to her feet and clutched the cold concrete wall while waiting for dizziness to pass. "This is the third time this week that I've almost died, not to mention my career total. But I'm alive and I have to move on to my next problem, which is the possibility of Mom knowing that I'm a vigilante. Death is easy compared to what my mother might do. Besides, doesn't Musashi say that the way of the warrior is resolute acceptance of death?"

She looked over at Karl and discovered he'd faded out again. Shaking her head in frustration, she walked over to the shrine where her sword stand sat in front of a small statue of Amida Buddha. She bowed and whispered the nembutsu, "Namu Amida Butsu," a few times before she placed the sword in its home.

She walked over to her backpack and peeled off her shirt and undershirt, savoring the feel of cool air against her sweaty skin. She tugged at the front of her sports bra to help with ventilation.

"I don't understand," Karl said. Jamie shrieked and threw her shirt at the intangible form of Karl. The spirit seemed too distracted to pay much attention to her. "I've never seen anything like this."

"Seen anything like what?" Jamie asked. Karl disappeared again without answering.

She had stripped out of her costume, treated all her cuts and scrapes, put on street clothes and choked down a protein bar before Karl appeared again.

"Is this what it's like for a spirit to run around like a chicken with its head cut off?" Jamie asked as she walked over to the mini-fridge and pulled out a carton of milk.

"What?" Karl asked, snapping out of his reverie.

"Nothing," Jamie said. "Just a joke."

She crouched down next to a saucer on the ground, legs threatening to give out underneath her. She poured the milk into a saucer and watched as the spirit of the lair padded into sight. Her hideout had once been a bolt hole for a superhero from the '70s named Devil Cat. The black and red feline that represented the spirit of the place still carried that energy.

"Oh. I do not understand your need to… quip."

Jamie fell back into a seated position and covered her face. "Look, I'm sorry. Long night. Natural-born smartass."

"May I ask a question?"

"Fire away," she said, turning to get her knees underneath her as she tried to stand.

"What do you call it when you cannot feel your hand?" Karl asked.

"Your hand falls asleep?" Jamie offered. "Or goes numb?"

"Yes. I have numb spots. We need to investigate it."

Jamie reached her feet and then leaned against the wall. Another wave of tears threatened her. She just couldn't cope any more. "No, you need to investigate. I need to get home before my mom wakes up, get a minute of sleep and try to stay awake tomorrow. I will try to help tomorrow."

Karl frowned and disappeared.

CHAPTER 2 - BOYS AND GIRLS

Jamie Hattori jerked awake. She'd fallen asleep leaning against her locker. As her eyes focused, she saw someone standing in front of her. The girl wore blue eye-shadow, bright red lipstick and rouge. It reminded Jamie of ravers she sometimes saw stumbling home at night. The girl's short hair had been dyed an unnatural shade of red and spiked up. She had a pale olive complexion that hinted at Mediterranean genes. Hanging from her ears were a pair of white disks long enough to touch the shoulders of her slightly too-small T-shirt featuring a man's face and the word "Bowie."

"Were you," Jamie croaked before clearing her throat. "Were you talking to me?"

The girl looked panicked. "Oh god, were you really asleep? I thought you were just zoning out. I'm so sorry!"

Jamie waved the apology aside. "Was there something you wanted?"

"Roller derby," the girl said. She hesitated before adding, "I was wondering if you were interested in roller derby."

Jamie looked around at the other students passing in the hallway, trying to figure out if this was some joke. Only a few people seemed to pay her any attention, mostly those who had lockers near Jamie. Very few were people who knew her. She spotted Sabrina Alvarez, the cheer captain, who looked away quickly when Jamie made eye contact. She saw a few other people she knew, some by face if not by name. Why was a raver from Mars asking her about... anything?

Jamie turned her attention back to the girl in front of her. "I'm sorry, did you say 'roller derby?'"

The girl's smile grew even more fragile. "Yes."

"I don't know." Jamie wiped at her chin in case she'd drooled while she nodded off. She didn't want to upset the girl or look like an idiot, but was certain she was doing both. "Why?"

"I was wondering if you'd like to go to a roller derby bout. The Goblin Town Roller Girls are playing this Friday. I thought you might like to go."

"Oh, you're selling tickets," Jamie said, relieved that this wasn't the beginning of a prank. "Sorry, I'm broke."

"No, I was just inviting you to come with me," the girl said. "Like, the two of us. I'm willing to buy."

This knocked Jamie back to confusion. "Okay. And who are you?"

"I guess you missed that part when you were sleeping. I'm Parker," the girl said, extending her hand. "Parker Fiorenza." Jamie reluctantly shook. Her hand was warm and soft in Jamie's.

Jamie didn't respond right away, her brain still fuzzy. She realized belatedly that she still held Parker's hand and pulled her hand back. "And where is this thing at?" Jamie was certain she was missing something and wondered if this was some sort of trap for her masked identity. For all Jamie knew, this could be the alter ego to some ridiculous villain named "The Raver." Or maybe just some weird prank by a social group she hadn't run afoul of yet. Did she piss off any ravers?

"West Key Community College," Parker said. "They have a new gymnasium and—"

"Right, West Key is a little far for me. I don't have a car, and the bus down there is a rolling psych ward at night."

"I have a car," Parker blurted out. "I can give you a ride."

Jamie frowned. "So why are you wanting to do all this for me?" Then something clicked in her sleep-deprived mind. "Wait, are you asking me out on a date?"

Parker opened her mouth to reply, but then shifted her gaze past Jamie's shoulder just as sounds of outrage began to rise above the general buzz of conversation. Jamie turned in time to see a fist flying at her face. She dodged the punch, even as her bruised ribs groaned in pain. The attack hit the locker behind her with a loud crash, and Jamie hurried down the hall, pushing Parker ahead of her.

"I'm going to kill you!" a male voice yelled out.

Jamie looked back to see a huge red-faced blonde guy in a Lincoln High letterman jacket clutching his fist in pain. She dimly recalled him being on the football team, and he definitely had the build for it. Conversation around them died, surprise stripping the other students of words.

The football player crouched down and charged at Jamie just as Parker tried to intervene. Jamie shoved Parker into the crowd, then turned to deal with the football player. Jamie couldn't stop his momentum, so she grabbed his injured hand as he drew near, stepped aside, and threw him past her. She almost collapsed as her knee protested the exertion. The jock collided with several onlookers, including Sabrina, who went tumbling with a high-pitched yelp. From behind, Jamie saw his name on his jacket: "Carmichael."

Jamie backed up and the crowd pulled away, stunned murmurs replacing the silence. The gossip from this fight would ruin her chances of maintaining her low profile at school, but she'd burn that bridge when she came to it. Carmichael shook his head like a dazed beast and pushed back up onto his feet.

"So, uh... Carmichael?" Jamie called out. "I think there's been some sort of mistake. I don't know who you are, but clearly you're upset about something. How about we talk this out?"

She couldn't believe he almost got the drop on her. Normally, the spirit of the school kept an eye open for her, and she lit incense and offered food for him whenever possible. But no sign of the spirit existed. This was beginning to look like a conspiracy.

The football player turned and walked towards her more slowly, hands in front of him like a wrestler. Jamie slipped into a defensive stance and tried to figure out how to deal with this. The hallway was too narrow to circle around him and the crowd ringing them limited her backward mobility. He kept his right hand close to his chest, the fingers not quite forming a fist. She formulated a plan.

She moved toward Carmichael fast and feinted with her right hand before punching him in his injured hand with her left. He roared in pain. She used his moment of distraction to throw a jab at his nose before she swung around his right side and kicked him in the back of the knee.

He didn't drop from the kick, but he staggered forward a few steps before wheeling around to face her again. She feinted a right hook again, followed by a feint to his right hand before punching him in the face with two rapid blows. He stumbled back a few steps, leaving his torso open, so she punched him in the ribs and circled around again.

He slowed down and grew more clumsy, so she just pegged him with repeated jabs while swatting away his feeble punches. All she had to do at this point was wear him down.

She only noticed that the crowd had grown silent when a man's voice yelled out, "Okay you two, break it up!"

Jamie stepped away from Carmichael, raised her hands up in surrender and turned to face the man. She realized that the voice was Principal Mueller.

"What's going on here?" the principal demanded, interposing himself between the two of them.

"He attacked me," Jamie said while pointing at the jock, who now had blood running from his nose and ears. As Principal Mueller turned to look at Carmichael, the young man fell over.

~

Carmichael glared at Jamie from his seat on the far side of the office lobby. His face was puffing up and bloody toilet paper stuck out from his nostrils. Nearby, the thin and elderly receptionist, Ms. Holmgren, typed away on her keyboard.

"Your name is Carmichael, right?" Jamie asked, curiosity killing her.

The football player continued his sullen staring.

"Why did you think you needed to punch my lights out?"

The receptionist paused her typing and cleared her throat. "You two are not supposed to be talking. We don't want another little incident on our hands."

"I just want to—" Jamie started to say.

"You'll need to wait for Principal Mueller to talk to you."

Jamie opened her mouth to protest, but Ms. Holmgren fixed her with a look that didn't invite argument. The girl shut her mouth and slumped back in her seat. With a thin-lipped smile, the receptionist turned back to typing.

The door to the principal's office opened and a few students exited before Principal Mueller came out and said, "Mr.

Carmichael, please come in."

The football player limped slowly across the lobby into the principal's office, continuing to glare at Jamie, leaving Jamie alone with Ms. Holmgren and the clacking of plastic keys. Jamie tried to kill time by reading the notices on the bulletin board.

One of the school counselors entered the office. "Donna?" he said. "Did you get a chance to get ahold of any of the new unexcused absences?"

"Yes, it's like the others. Their parents don't know where their children are and have contacted the police."

Jamie didn't realize what she had heard for a few moments, then whipped her gaze around to the reception desk.

Ms. Holmgren broke off from talking to the counselor to meet Jamie's gaze. "Yes?"

"Just wondering what you're talking about," Jamie said.

"I'm certain it's none of your business." Ms. Holmgren turned back to the counselor and spoke more quietly.

Jamie turned away and whispered urgently, "Karl? Are you there?"

A few moments later, Karl stood next to her. He fidgeted, uncharacteristically anxious. "I've been trying to figure out—"

"Not right now," Jamie interrupted, still whispering. "Can't talk much now. What do you know about the missing kids?"

"What missing kids?"

"The missing kids from my school."

Karl looked down and frowned. "This... this isn't... I'll be back." He disappeared, as though he had never been there.

"You shouldn't be talking on your cell phone, young lady," Ms. Holmgren said, pausing in her typing.

Jamie turned toward the receptionist and held up her hands to show she had no cell phone, then turned her head to show a lack of earbuds. Ms. Holmgren narrowed her eyes in annoyance. As she typed, she continued glancing furtively at Jamie.

The door opened and Carmichael exited with the principal behind him. "Go ahead and have a seat again, Mr. Carmichael. Miss Hattori, will you please join me."

Carmichael glared at her again as he passed her. She met his gaze and then turned her attention to the principal.

Principal Mueller closed the door behind her then went over to sit behind his desk. "Have a seat, Miss Hattori."

Jamie sat down and looked over at the principal expectantly.

"Care to tell me what happened with you and Steven?" Principal Mueller asked as he glanced at his computer monitor. Jamie couldn't see what was on the screen from her angle, but something about the monitor nagged at her vision.

"Who?"

"Steven Carmichael. The boy you beat up."

"Sorry, he didn't tell me his name before he ambushed me."

"A smart attitude will not help your situation, young lady."

Jamie shrugged. "I was talking to a girl named Parker about roller derby. I heard a commotion behind me. I turned in time to see him coming at me, and I defended myself."

"And what did you do to provoke the attack?" He glanced back at the monitor.

"Nothing, as far I can tell. Unless my very existence offends him on some level."

"So you're going to tell me you didn't spread rumors about his athletic performance?"

Jamie raised her hands in frustration. "I didn't know the guy's name until he showed up all angry. Why would I spread rumors about him?"

"That's what I'm asking you."

She rolled her eyes. "Why don't you ask the person he allegedly heard it from?"

"It was on a blog that publishes school gossip. We don't know who runs it."

"Then I don't know what to tell you. I've never said anything about him. I did nothing to provoke him."

Principal Mueller focused his attention on the monitor. "It says here that you said, and I quote, 'Steven Carmichael is the worst thing to happen to the Lincoln High Loggers varsity football team, and the coaches know it. It's no surprise that they're looking to cut him before the homecoming game.' Are you telling me that you never said that?"

Jamie slumped in her chair and looked up at the textured ceiling tiles. "Yes. That is what I'm telling you. Wait a second, is that the blog you're looking at?"

Jamie rocked up out of her seat and leaned over his desk to look at the screen. Principal Mueller shoved his chair back hard and scrambled away from her. The blog was titled "2 the Fairest" and featured a golden apple for a logo. The letters on the apple looked a lot like the ones from the apple she had found in the alley the night before. She scanned for her name but the surface of the screen seemed to ripple in front of her, as though something writhed beneath the glowing image on the screen. She could feel anger rising at the thought of someone doing this to her. She could just hit someone—

"Miss Hattori, get back in your seat!" the principal yelled. Jamie realized that he'd said it a few times and his voice kept getting more shrill.

She pulled herself out of her daze, flopped back into her seat, and scowled at the back of the computer. She caught motion again and focused. She thought she could see worms again, but her concentration was broken by the door opening.

Ms. Holmgren poked her head in, eyes wide. "Is everything alright in here? I heard you yelling."

"Just fine, Donna," the principal said, straightening his tie and sitting back down at his computer.

Ms. Holmgren glared at Jamie. "Very well, sir." She closed the door and her footsteps could be heard walking back across the office.

Principal Mueller cleared his throat and glanced at his computer again before focusing on Jamie. "You will be suspended for three days, and I will be requesting a meeting with your parents."

"Wait, what?" Jamie sat up straight, her heart racing in shock. This was going to be hard to explain to her mom. "I'm being suspended? For being attacked?"

"You are being suspended for fighting."

"But he attacked me!" Jamie rose out of her seat, but sat back down when she saw the expression of fear on the principal's face. "Just so I know what to tell my parents, am I being punished for not being an athlete or not being white?"

Principal Mueller closed his eyes with a pained expression on his face. "It is school policy for us to suspend both people involved in the fight. It's covered in our Student Code of Conduct, which you can find on our Website. It takes two people to fight."

"So I'm just supposed to let him pound on me?"

The principal opened his mouth, then paused for a moment. "You know, I am not going to debate this with you. I will talk to your parents about school policy, not you. Our conversation is done here. You can wait in the lobby for your parents to come pick you up from school."

CHAPTER 3 - HOME LIFE

Jamie's dad, Charles, followed her out to the car with a stern look on his face. Jamie knew he was just waiting until they got inside the car to talk to her, and she didn't want to hear it. But she knew she'd have to deal with this sooner or later.

She didn't look at her father as they each got into the car. He put his key in the ignition but didn't turn it. Silence hung between them. Jamie broke the silence.

"Will you just get it out of your system, Dad?" She looked out the window, not wanting to see the look on his face.

Charles took a deep breath and released it before saying, "A football player, huh?"

Jamie said, "Yes."

"Like how big?"

"Six foot? Couple hundred pounds?"

"Knocked him out?"

"He collapsed, I didn't investigate."

"You get a picture of what he looked like afterwards?"

Jamie rested her head against the glass. "I was a little busy."

"I'll have to check the Internet," her father mused as he started the car. "I'm sure someone with a camera phone must have gotten it."

"Dad, this isn't something to geek out about."

"Are you kidding? My little girl took out a linebacker or something. That's so cool! Maybe he'll become part of your rogues' gallery." He shook the steering wheel in his excitement.

"My what?"

"Rogues' gallery. The usual roster of villains a superhero faces."

"You are such an embarrassing dork that it hurts my soul." Jamie was glad she hadn't told him about her power. She wouldn't be able to live under the same roof with him.

"Oh, come on! And here your mom fusses about putting you in martial arts at three. It's one thing to know you're secretly a superhero, another thing to have documented proof that my daughter's a badass."

Jamie turned and faced her father. "And when she discovers that I'm wearing a mask and chasing bad guys around with a katana that I stole from you?"

Her dad nodded and more quietly said, "Okay. Yeah, there's that. We can try and soften the blow. You could spend the day studying in your room."

"Actually, I was wondering if I could get dropped off at the church. Sensei wanted me to do some stuff around the place and I might as well take care of it before the hammer hits. I can hit the books when I get home."

"If that's what you want." Her dad shrugged.

He glanced to the right and slammed on the brakes. Ten feet ahead a caped figure hurtled uncontrollably across the street, his clothing on fire, and crashed through a wooden fence. A woman of living flame flew after him, but her caped quarry stood as she arrived and shot at her with some sort of energy gun. She answered with fiery blasts and the two continued down the street like that. In the yard where they crashed, the family stepped out of their house and looked around in muted shock. The spirit of the yard ran around in confusion, unsure how to deal with the damage.

Her dad looked around to make sure the coast was clear, then began driving forward again. "Did you recognize either of them?"

Jamie shook her head. "No. They must be new in town."

"I'll have to check out the news when this blows over. Figure out who the criminal was. Of course, your mother will probably be blogging about this." Charles frowned and shook his head. He drove in silence for several minutes, his attention only barely on the road. Jamie hated when her dad was like this.

"Let's be fair," Jamie said. "It could be just a domestic dispute."

Charles burst out laughing, shaking him out of his dark mood. "Man, I feel bad for the cop that has to break up that sort of domestic violence situation." He laughed a bit more and shook his head. "So, anyway. What was this Steven guy's beef with you anyway?"

"I don't know. Someone claimed on a gossip blog that I had trash-talked his football reputation."

"Jackass. Good thing he messed with you and not someone who couldn't fight."

Jamie sighed. "Thanks, Dad."

~

Jamie walked up the steps to the Cobalt City Buddhist Church and waved distractedly to her father as he drove away. "Karl? You around?"

No response came from Karl. This was becoming increasingly weird.

Halfway up, one of the church's two guardian spirits materialized next to her. He looked like a Japanese man except red, seven feet tall and built like a body builder. He wore only a pair of loose silk pants and carried a *vajra* club slung over one shoulder. He always scowled.

"Hey kid," the spirit said.

"Hey Agyo," Jamie said back. "How's the guardian spirit business?"

"Slow. Not a whole lot of greed, hatred or delusion being aimed at us lately." The spirit shook his head. "People are too wishy-washy and PC these days. I would love to smash my club into the face of a greed spirit. They're so sleazy. But no, just the usual locals. They're a bit deluded, but it's just not the same. The angels guarding the Methodist church down the street are getting harder to rile up and I still don't know what to do with the angel over at the Unitarian place. Weirdo."

On reaching the door, Jamie fished her keys out of her pocket and let herself into the church. She'd started volunteering a month ago when her parents were on her about getting a job. The minister trusted her and had given her the run of the place so she could work around her schedule.

"I hear there's a Unitarian Jihad," Jamie said.

"Really?" Agyo asked, stopping to look back towards the Unitarian Church. "He hides it well. What does it take to get the jihad aimed at you?"

"Vote by committee, I think," Jamie said. Just inside the door she saw the other spirit, Ungyo, standing guard in the entry way. He looked much like Agyo, but never spoke and carried a sword instead of a club. While Agyo kept evil out of the church, Ungyo kept the good in.

Agyo scowled for a moment. "Wait, is this a joke?"

Jamie pointed a finger back at the spirit and smiled. "Gotcha."

"Jamie, is that you?" the familiar voice of Reverend Nishijima called from down the hall.

"Yes, Sensei," Jamie replied.

The minister poked his head out of the door to the office. "Is someone with you? I thought I heard you talking to someone."

"No, Sensei. I'm just... reciting the *nembutsu*."

"Really?" Reverend Nishijima asked, adjusting the thick black frames of his glasses. Agyo and Ungyo continued down the hall past the minister, unseen and unheard by the mortal man. "I could have sworn I heard the word 'jihad.'"

"Nope. Just me saying 'Namu Amida Butsu' over and over again. I could see how you'd mistake 'Amida' for 'jihad.'"

"Jamie, don't compare Amida Buddha to the jihad." He withdrew back into the office only to stick his head out again a second later. "What are you doing here so early? Don't you have school right now?"

"Oh yeah," Agyo blurted out. "What are you doing here so early?"

Jamie squirmed as the physical and spiritual gazes pinned her down. "Yeah, funny thing about that. I got sort of suspended. For fighting."

Ungyo placed the palm of his hand on his face and shook his head. Agyo thrust a fist in the air. "Yes!"

Reverend Nishijima frowned. "Jamie, I'm very disappointed in you. Do your parents know about this?"

"Dad knows. He got the call to pick me up. Dropped me off here so I could get in some extra work time. I get to face Mom's wrath tonight."

Reverend Nishijima withdrew back into the office. "It's just as well that you're here. I can't for the life of me find the minutes from the meeting we had yesterday."

"They're behind the desk," Agyo said. "They fell back there this morning when he was clearing some other stuff off."

19

"Maybe they fell behind the desk?" Jamie said as she came up to the door. "Just a hunch."

The business office for the church was a small cluttered room, just big enough for a desk and a couple old filing cabinets. Reverend Nishijima stood leaning over the desk, his head resting against the wall. "Oh, hey, I think I see it there. I don't know what I'd do without your hunches. It's like you know this place inside and out."

Jamie headed into the church proper to bow before Amida Buddha, offer some incense and bow again as she left. Since her power had awakened, she had felt a new power from the statue of Amida Buddha, but never an actual spirit of the statue. The more she saw of the city, the less she understood how the rules for spirits worked.

Jamie returned to the office just as Reverend Nishijima climbed off the desk and blew dust bunnies off of the notebook.

"Mind if I use the computer in here real quick before I get cracking on other stuff?" Jamie asked.

The minister nodded distractedly as he wandered towards the door with the notes. "Sure thing. I have to take this over to Reverend Smith, so you have a bit of time before I need the office again."

Jamie plopped into the chair, opened a browser window and entered "2 the fairest" into the search engine. The first to pop up was the website 2thefairest.com. Beneath that were links to an online encyclopedia article which caught Jamie's eye: "Apple of Discord." This was followed by another article in the same encyclopedia and a bunch of random inclusions of the word "fairest." Jamie clicked on the blog link first.

The most recent blog post was dated the day before.

Jamie Hattori Outs Steven Carmichael as the Logger Football Team's Weakest Link

Lincoln High Senior Jamie Hattori was overheard in the cafeteria at lunch to say that she had it on good authority that Steven Carmichael, running back for the Lincoln Loggers, was inches from being cut from the team due to gross incompetence. He's spent weeks on the bench and Jamie says it's a sign of things to come.

"Steven Carmichael is the worst thing to happen to the Lincoln High Loggers varsity football team, and the coaches know it," Jamie said. "It's

no surprise that they're looking to cut him before the homecoming game."

Jamie glared at the monitor, chest tight, jaw clenched, blood roaring in her ears. She had never said such a thing. She didn't even care about football. She was going to find that Carmichael and throttle him for believing that she—

A cold draft blew through her mind and cleared away her rage. As her mind cleared, she noticed Ungyo's sword in front of her face and Agyo's club in front of the monitor.

"Okay, did something weird just happen?"

"There's some sort of magic coming from the website," Agyo said, eyes locked on screen. "I wish the person who did this was here. Then I'd give him a thrashing."

Jamie focused on the spiritual aspect of the website and could see black worms writhing just past the monitor. "This makes the second worm-filled 'apple' I've come across in less than twenty-four hours. And both of them were tied to someone making my life miserable."

"It's the Apple of Discord," Agyo clarified. "Turn off the computer. It will take some time for the spell to dissipate."

Jamie closed the browser window and shut down the computer. Both spirits slumped forward a moment later, as though some wall had disappeared. "Okay, so what's the Apple of Discord?"

"It has to do with Eris." Agyo straightened up and sat on the edge of the desk. "Greek goddess of strife. According to legend, all of Olympus had been invited to a royal wedding except for Eris. To get back at them she threw a golden apple into the wedding party with 'to the fairest' written on it. Or *'Kallisti'* if you want the original Greek. Three of the goddesses claimed it should belong to them. One thing led to another, and so you had the Trojan War and the fall of Troy."

"How do you know that?" Jamie asked.

"The church library has a copy of *Bulfinch's Mythology.* Just because I'm slow doesn't mean I'm dumb." Agyo crossed his arms across his chest, every muscle seeming to bulge even more.

"Fine. Sorry. So those weird letters on the apple are Greek for 'to the fairest?' So someone with magic and a thing for Greek mythology has targeted me? Why?"

"You're one of the few superheroes in Karlsburg these days, aren't you? You could be standing in the way of someone's criminal enterprise. This could be your arch-nemesis."

"I don't think I rate an arch-nemesis."

"This could be your big break!"

"I hate this job." Jamie shoved her chair back and stalked out the door.

~

Jamie sat at her desk, the music of AKB48 blasting from her earbuds while she read her algebra textbook. Or, tried to read. Really she just stared at the word "quadratic" while she brooded over how badly her mom was going to react to finding out she had been in a fight.

Light poured into the room as her dad opened the door. Jamie pulled one earbud out and looked over.

"Your mom wants you downstairs," her dad said. He sounded tired, and she imagined he'd already gone a few rounds in her defense. Gloria Hattori's temper was the thing of legends. "She's been yelling for you for a while. I told her I'd get you."

Jamie thumbed off her MP3 player and followed him out of the room. As she trudged down the stairs, the smell of roast beef filled her nostrils. The strident voice of anti-superhero pundit Lyle Prather came from the TV in the living room. Jamie winced, hating to talk to her mom when she was charged up by her favorite pundit.

Jamie's dad stepped aside when he reached the bottom of the stairs, leaving a path for her straight to the living room. Jamie hesitated a moment before rounding the corner to face her mom. From where she stood, Jamie could see the empty display rack where her father's katana had once rested—before Jamie stole it. The spirit of the house, a *zashiki-warashi*, sat at the bottom of the stairs. It looked like a six year old child, half black and half Japanese, with a reddish tint to its features. It looked up at Jamie with wide, tear-filled eyes. The look on the spirit's face said all she needed to know about how bad this was going to be.

Jamie took the final few steps into the living room. Gloria stood there, jaw clenched, nostrils flared and eyes glaring at her daughter. Jamie looked more like her mother than her father. Her eyes came from her dad's Japanese heritage, but her skin tone and hair came from her African-American mom. But while Jamie opted for dreadlocks, Gloria straightened her hair.

Jamie met her mom's gaze for a few moments before looking down to the ground. She knew her mom would disown her if Jamie's role as Kensei came to light. And Jamie knew she wouldn't stop, regardless of consequences.

Neither spoke right away. The only sound came from the TV, as Prather ranted. "To this day," he yelled, "We still don't know where the money came from to support the multi-billion dollar fortress the Icons and the Protectorate used. Jaccob Stevens probably funded some of it, but what sort of other shadowy backers were behind it?"

Finally Jamie's mom asked, "What were you thinking?"

"I was thinking I was defending myself," Jamie mumbled.

"Speak up and look at me when I'm talking to you. What were you thinking?"

Jamie looked up into her mom's baleful gaze. "I was defending myself."

"What did you do to provoke him?"

Jamie wanted to yell that it wasn't her fault, but all she could manage was a weak, "Nothing."

"So someone attacked you just because?"

"Someone," Jamie's voice cracked and she stopped to clear her throat. "Someone claimed I said something I didn't. It was some rumor about this guy, and he blamed me for the rumor."

"Why would someone stir something up against you?"

Jamie didn't dare say the probable truth: Because she ran around in a mask and beat up criminals in the neighborhood. Instead she just mumbled, "I don't know." She repeated it louder when her mom looked like she was about to yell again.

"Is it drugs?" her mom asked. "Or did you join a gang?"

Jamie fought off the urge to laugh, since her mom would probably prefer that to the truth. Instead she just said, "No."

"You should have run," her mom said. "You have no right to take the law into your own hands." Jamie winced at her mom using one of Prather's stock arguments. "Your father insisted on having you do all those martial arts classes, but that doesn't mean you have to use it. If you are so good that you can take out a football player, a *football player*, you are good enough to get away and let the proper authorities take care of this."

Jamie had no answer for that.

23

"This had better be the last time I have to hear that you've been—" Jamie's mom stopped as she heard what Prather was saying on the television. Her eyes focused on the screen. Jamie also looked at the image of the man, his graying curly hair looking just as crazy as always. The bottom of the screen showed that Prather had gone into his "Masks in the News" segment.

"Jaccob Stevens, better known as the armored vigilante Stardust, was seen destroying property last night in yet another unnecessary attempt to aid duly appointed officers of the law in stopping a crime. I can only hope that Stevens' bottomless pockets empty out from all his property damage fines. The last thing we need is a repeat of the damage from the Protectorate War five years ago."

The strong-jawed pundit disappeared as news footage from the attacks filled the screen. A giant worm blasted the street with an energy beam from its maw as it followed a red car. The glint of golden armor flew over the site and blasted the car as well. Asphalt and neighboring cars burned in the wake of the attacks. Jamie had seen this footage before. In the corner was Prather's logo for "The Protectorate War," a term he coined after things went bad.

The Protectorate had been the A-list superhero group at the time. One day they turned on one another and destroyed huge swaths of downtown in their conflict. Afterwards, the Protectorate had held a press conference to explain that some of their team had been replaced with imposters. It was weird, but not implausible in a place like Cobalt City. Things were fine for a while, and then the gang wars broke out. Some people, like Prather, claimed the Protectorate had been backing the gang wars as part of their own internal conflicts. All Jamie knew was that when the dust had settled, many superheroes had died or gone missing. The remaining members of the Protectorate disbanded under a cloud of suspicion. Most of them left town.

Gloria had watched all the news reports after her father, Jamie's Grandpa Brown, had died during that first conflict. His car had been one of many that had been destroyed in the explosive blasts from the villains that allegedly impersonated Stardust and the Worm Queen. They never outright saw his car blow up in the footage that Prather now replayed, but they knew it had been nearby.

"Casualties were high during this assault on the city," Prather said as the footage continued. "My wife and sons were among them. Many others who lost loved ones or who barely survived the attacks have shared their tragedy, so I know that I am not alone in my grieving. The souls of our loved ones will never rest until those who hide behind false names and work outside of due process of law are brought to justice."

"Get out of my sight," Jamie's mom whispered, tears streaming down her face.

Jamie edged away from her mom and ran up the stairs to her room.

CHAPTER 4 - BACK ON THE STREET

The security guard rolled by on his Segway, patrolling the perimeter. Kensei watched as he passed—waiting for him to gain some distance before she ran across the street—then launched herself up the side of the ten-foot-high chain-link fence and scrambled up and over it. She hit the other side at a run and kept her head low. From the edge of her vision, she saw the light from the guard's flashlight pan over the patch of fence she'd just jumped.

She couldn't believe it was this hard to break into a high school. Normally she had help, but the spirit of the school wasn't responding to her summons from outside, so this required access to the heart of matters.

Kensei noticed the flashlight beam tracking through the area she had just passed. She ducked behind a large, boxy HVAC unit that stood a few feet from the wall of the school building. A moment later a beam of light passed over her head, and she heard footsteps. He must have abandoned the Segway. She couldn't believe she was getting this much grief from a rent-a-cop. Was she getting sloppy or was he just the Sherlock Holmes of security guards?

As he drew closer, she maneuvered around to keep the HVAC between her and the guard. It took a few laps before he gave up and left the area. As soon as he rounded the corner, Kensei scrambled up a drain pipe to the rooftop and ran in a low crouch to the roof of the gymnasium. She paused at the top, letting the pain in her ribs and joints abate before she moved again.

There she found the shrine she had built from cast-off Lincoln High Logger paraphernalia. It included foam "#1" fingers, a log cabin built from "Lincoln High Logger" pencils, a waterproof blanket that formed the roof to the shrine, and the centerpiece: a bobblehead of the school mascot, Abe the Lincoln Logger. The mascot was designed to look like a caricature of Abraham Lincoln, dressed all in flannel. The smell of rancid milk and spoiled fruit wafted up from the saucer in front of the bobblehead. Spirits loved the offerings, but the mess was foul.

"Abe?" Kensei called out. "Where are you?"

"Don't you normally offer milk before you call on me?" Abe asked. Kensei turned to face the spirit. He looked much older than the toy, and uncomfortable in the flannel. The school had changed mascots a few times, from the original Braves to the Red Devils to the Loggers. The spirit didn't seem to adapt well to the changes.

"The offering was for you to warn me of any danger. You didn't give me a heads up when an angry jock came looking to cave my face in."

"When did this happen?" Abe asked, his expression stiff and reserved. Kensei read it as his attempt to look sincere.

"Don't play dumb with me, Abe. Does this have something to do with a blogger that loves golden apples?"

Abe flinched and looked away.

Kensei sighed. This wasn't something she wanted to be right about. "You're a lousy liar, Honest Abe. So what happened?"

"Someone had a more compelling offer," the spirit muttered.

"What, they're putting whipping cream and organic fruit in your bowl?" Kensei leaned around to look Abe in the eye, but he turned the other way to avoid her gaze.

"She is capable of hurting me."

"So it's a 'she'? What else can you tell me?"

Abe looked at Kensei in wide-eyed alarm. "Part of my agreement is that I remain quiet about her."

"What if I raise the quality of the offerings? Or take them away entirely?"

Abe shrugged and slouched. "It wouldn't matter. The offerings are nice, but I gain more sustenance from pep rallies. She could tear this school apart and me with it. You can't compete."

Desperate, Kensei asked, "Well, what if I tore the school apart more than she could?"

The spirit grunted a bitter laugh. "I know you well enough to know you could never do that, even if you had the same power she does."

"Campus Security," a man called out. "Come out where I can see you!" The spirit faded from sight and Kensei dropped low. The flashlight beam chased her from one hiding place to another until she reached the edge of the roof and jumped off.

~

The boy ahead of Kensei shoved a garbage can across the alleyway to slow her. She vaulted over it and continued the chase. Spirits of the buildings poked their heads through the walls on either side. Even in the dark of the alley, they stood out. Unfortunately, the small bits of debris were less obvious. The only consolation Kensei had was that the person she chased stumbled more than she did.

He shot out of the end of the alley into the street and was greeted by the blare of a car horn as it screeched to a stop next to him. He stumbled in surprise, for a moment staring wide-eyed into the headlights. Kensei tripped over a box in the darkness, making enough racket to break him from his reverie. He turned and continued running into the next alleyway. The car resumed moving forward, blocking Kensei's path. She scrambled up the metal side, to the roof and then jumped off the far side after her quarry.

She had tried returning to the alley where she had been ambushed the night before and speaking to the spirit, but it had ignored her summons. Kensei was about to give up when she spotted a face she recalled from the ambush. She chased and he ran.

She'd seen him around the neighborhood before. He might even attend her school, not that she actually talked to her classmates. Mostly she recognized him because he was a low-rent crook that the real criminals wouldn't take seriously. His biggest crimes usually involved disorderly conduct and unsuccessfully mugging little old ladies. He clearly wasn't in the best physical condition, as he was already starting to stumble from exhaustion.

Ahead of her, there was a blur of motion and a wet crunching sound. She slid to a halt and looked down the alley for any sign of her quarry. Kensei heard slurping and saw someone new crouched over the body of her target. She drew her sword and stalked forward. As she approached, the crouching person stood and turned to face her while licking his lips.

He was skinnier and shorter than Kensei, and acne marred his pale skin. His mouth and chin were stained red and droplets streaked down his neck. He smiled and displayed red teeth with chunks of raw meat stuck in his braces. Blood poured out of his victim's neck.

"It isn't nice to sneak up on people, even if you're a ninja," he said. Kensei remembered seeing him in the halls at Lincoln High, his bright red hair drawing a lot of attention. "What are you supposed to be? Some sort of superhero?"

"Yes," Kensei said as she swung her left fist at his face. She pulled her punch some, not wanting to break him. But he barely budged when she connected with his jaw and the impact sent a jolt of pain up her arm.

He laughed, snorting as he did so. "Is that the best you got?"

"No." Kensei kneed him in the crotch, not holding anything back.

He stopped laughing. While he hunched over, she hit him with an uppercut that left him sprawled on his back. Her hand ached from the punch, but she wasn't about to let this guy see her hurt.

"You bitch!" he gasped as he stood up. "Do you know who I am?"

"World's lamest vampire?" she asked as she aimed the blade of her katana at his face.

She saw him tense, signaling his intention to charge long before he actually did. But she wasn't ready for how fast he could move or how strong he was. He batted her sword out of line and was nearly on her before she shifted out of the way. He still caught her with a glancing blow and the two of them fell to the concrete. Kensei vaulted from her back to her feet and pulled back to give herself more room. As she moved, she splashed through a puddle of something. She didn't want to think about what it could be.

"I am a creature of the night!" he screamed, lunging forward with his hands extended. "You will learn your place in the food chain."

Kensei swatted at his hands with the tip of her sword and he shrieked and pulled back. The smell of burning meat filled the air.

She heard the spirit of the sword laugh with smug delight.

"Magic laughing sword, huh?" he asked as he stepped away. Kensei tensed, not used to others being able to hear spirits. "Well, you have to sleep sometime, ninja girl."

"The name's Kensei," she said.

That seemed to confuse him. "What? Like from *Oriental Adventures?*"

"I don't know what you're talking about." Kensei walked towards him. "But I think I should be offended."

"Another time, Kensei!" He turned and spread his arms, his body blurring and shrinking as he turned into an owl in flight.

"Aren't you supposed to be a bat?" she yelled. The owl shrieked and flew off into the night. She re-sheathed her katana and muttered, "If this is what it's like to have a rogues' gallery, I'm going to file a complaint. So, sword. Any idea why he could hear you?"

The sword didn't answer.

"You suck."

She turned and looked at the boy she'd been chasing. He lay like a marionette with its strings cut, limbs sticking out in all directions, his neck a mess of shredded meat. Blood soaked his clothes and began to pool up underneath him. She could sense that his soul had moved on and all that was left was a dead body missing half its throat. The spirit of the alley, a starving and battered little girl, crouched beside the body. Blood spattered her face and dress. She looked up at Kensei with accusing eyes.

Kensei swallowed hard, trying to ignore the look on the spirit's face. She knew the spirit just wanted someone to blame and Kensei was convenient, but she didn't like it. Spirits of the stores that the alley ran between came out and began talking to one another. They moaned about property values and whether this would scare off customers, just as all store spirits did.

She turned and went in search of a pay phone to call the police. Better he was found by them than someone taking out their garbage.

~

Mike O'Reilly left the apartment building, still shouting curses at his wife three stories up. Kensei didn't know if Mike's wife,

Stephanie, could actually hear her husband, but the vigilante could hear the muffled voice of Mrs. O'Reilly shouting her own stream of insults back. When he was on the sidewalk, he finally stopped yelling and just muttered to himself. The spirit of the apartment building lingered on the front stoop, arms wrapped protectively about itself as it glared at Mike accusingly.

Up on the rooftop, Kensei kept pace with Mike, watching for an opportunity. He made a beeline for the nearest liquor store, went inside and eventually came back out with a large paper bag. Assuming he'd take the same route back, she ran ahead and waited for him in the darkness of an alley.

Even in the dim light, she could see the alley's spirit, emaciated with knobby knees and elbows, shaking its head and whispering, "Please, no." This alley was a common place for muggings and other assaults. Kensei didn't like bringing more violence to this place, but she needed to understand what was going on in her neighborhood.

As Mike passed the mouth of the alley, Kensei threw a pebble and pegged him in the head. He gave a shout of alarm and looked around. "Who the hell did that?"

Kensei answered with another pebble, making sure he knew they came from the alley.

"No one messes with Mike O'Reilly," he declared as he barged into the alley.

Kensei withdrew into her patch of darkness, waiting for him to pass her. Once he was clear, she stepped out and drew her sword, placing the blade of the katana against the back of his neck.

"Mike O'Reilly," she said, trying to sound more confident than she felt. "You've got a lot of explaining to do."

"What are you, twelve?" he asked, starting to turn.

That stung. She kicked him in the back of the knee and he fell to his hands and knees with a grunt of pain. His bag hit the ground with the sound of breaking glass, and the smell of malt liquor filled the air. He had a good hundred pounds on her, and a lot of it muscle. Kensei had seen him in enough parking lot scuffles to know he was lousy in a fight. But if he got his hands on her, she'd be in trouble.

"I'm asking the questions, O'Reilly," she said.

He glanced back at her and tried to make out what she looked like in the darkness. "Who the hell are you?"

"You attacked me last night," Kensei said. "I should think you know me already."

"Attacked you?" he asked, rising. Kensei slashed at the back of his thigh, cutting through his jeans to leave him with a bleeding but shallow gash in the back of his leg. He fell, landing on his face. "Ah, damn it! I fell asleep in front of the TV last night! Just had some weird dream about chasing a ninja out of my neighborhood. Probably too much Chinese food and chopsocky movies."

"That was no dream," Kensei said, kicking him in the crotch from behind. He gurgled and fell onto his side. "Who put you up to it?"

"No one," he gasped as he pulled his knees up to his chest. "Oh, man. Did some supervillain put the whammy on me? Someone left an apple on my doorstep. Had something weird carved into it. I thought it might be Arabic so I brought it in and told Steph that I should call Homeland Security. Are the Muslims after me?"

The spirit of the alley drew up close to Kensei, hands clutched to its mouth as it sobbed. "Please, you have what you want. Will you please just stop this?"

Guilt stabbed at Kensei, but she tried to ignore it. She did this for a good reason, and it's not like Mike was a saint. She stepped quietly away and disappeared into the darkness. Behind her, she heard Mike and the spirit sobbing.

CHAPTER 5 - 2THEFAIREST

Jamie paused on the threshold of the café, letting the buzz of conversation and the smell of coffee fill her senses. A few people paused in their talk and turned to look at her, but she pretended not to notice and headed over to the cash register. School had gotten out half an hour earlier and the place was packed with high school students.

She always felt a little weird going into Shambalah Coffee House. It served as one of the few public places where minors in the area could hang out for prolonged periods of time, but she wasn't really the type who hung out with her peers.

On top of that, the place was swarming with cat spirits that only she could sense. Most buildings had some sort of guardian spirit, sometimes even a few depending on the type of building. But she never saw any obvious guardian spirit at Shambalah. Just a bunch of spirit cats that lay on all the surfaces and went through the motions of rubbing against things even though they were intangible.

But she liked the coffee, and the barista was nice, so she put up with a little weirdness and mostly only visited in off hours, usually to get some homework done when her parents were fighting. But the need to find someone who might have a lead on the gossip blog brought her in during the after school rush. Normally, she'd just ask Karl, but she hadn't been able to get ahold of Karl since the day before. She felt blind without him watching her back.

At the counter, the barista, Dave, straightened up from his

slouch. Dave was the prettiest man Jamie had ever met, with a slim androgynous face and silky fine hair. New customers mistook him for a woman until they came closer.

"The usual?" he asked.

"Yeah," she said. She opened her mouth to speak again but stopped as a wave of unease crashed over her and the bell on the door rang to announce another customer.

A cacophony of growls and hisses rose from the spiritual cats. She looked over to see Louis Malenfant come through the entrance and make a beeline straight for her. Karl had once told her that Malenfant was the avatar for a dark god. Jamie had glimpsed that power when she'd tricked a band of criminals into attacking him instead of her. He looked harmless physically with his widow's peak and pot belly, but the jaundiced miasma of madness poured off him into the spiritual realm. Jamie found it telling that few ever called him by his first name. His surname, which meant "bad child" in French, said it all.

"Hello, Louis," Dave said with a smile, oblivious to the fact that metaphorical crazy was leaking out onto the spiritual floor of the coffee shop. "Steamed milk?"

"What?" Malenfant asked. "Oh, yes. Here, I think I've got enough here." He tossed a few crumpled bills on the counter and turned back to Jamie. "I need to talk to you."

"Are you going to tell me you're doing weird magic stuff with apples and Greek writing?"

Malenfant frowned. On the spiritual level, she could hear tiny silver bells ringing and smell fetid water wafting off a long-dead lake. "I've been looking for you for days and I'm not in the mood for… whatever ridiculous pop culture thing you're going on about. I have a problem with a god and I need you to fix it."

Jamie froze, her heart pounding in her ears. He didn't want Jamie. He wanted Kensei. "Can we not talk about this here?" she whispered, clasping her hands together.

Malenfant looked about at the coffee shop and the teenagers staring at them, as though this was the first time he realized where he was. He shook his head, grabbed Jamie by the arm with more strength than one would expect and dragged her to the nearest available booth. She stumbled along behind him.

"I'll bring your drinks out to you," Dave called out.

Jamie sat opposite Malenfant. He grabbed the salt shaker from the condiment tray, unscrewed the cap, and poured out a design on the table. She could feel more than see the magical power bubble up from the sigil and expand out around them. As it passed through her, Jamie felt like something oily slid across her skin. Sound outside of their area dimmed. The few people that were curious about Malenfant no longer looked towards him.

"So, you're having trouble with a god?"

"Yes, and I need you to do something about it."

Jamie fumbled for words, hoping for divine intervention. "I don't mean to sound rude, but aren't you a god? Can't you just counter-god this god or something?"

"I am a completely different sort of being than this memetic parasite. I have other, more important things to do than deal with this annoyance. If you can recommend a different superhero in the area, possibly one who has a driver's license, I'll gladly go to them instead. But this creature is persistent and I do not have the time to deal with this."

Dave set down their drinks. The dimness of vision and sound for the rest of the coffee shop persisted, but while he stood next to them, Dave seemed part of the shared bubble. Malenfant looked startled by the intrusion.

"Enjoy your drinks, guys," Dave said and returned to the front counter.

"I hate that man," Malenfant said.

Jamie didn't like the tone of this conversation. "So, what? You just sic superheroes onto bad guys you don't like?"

"You are hardly one to criticize someone for siccing bad guys on someone, if you remember. But yes, for me it worked with the Protectorate until they got to know me better. You owe me this, Hattori. Yes, I know your name. After you dragged a band of criminals into my house, I went through great effort to learn all about you. I know your name, I know where you live. Should you be unwilling to handle this threat and I am forced to sully my hands, I can deal with it and your family."

Jamie shrugged and tried to maintain bravado. "Well, I guess if you're willing to come into a teen hangout with all your evil majesty, then this must be serious. Can you at least tell me what god this is?"

"A trickster god of some sort. It covers up its tracks well, so I don't have much else."

Jamie dreaded the thought that came to mind. "Could it be Greek?"

Malenfant rolled his eyes. "I didn't check its passport. Do you have some problem with Greeks?"

"Someone else has been causing me trouble, and they have this whole 'Eris' thing going on."

The avatar of the dark god paused and tilted his head as though listening to something. "Yes, I believe it is Eris. There. This should be much easier for you."

He picked up his drink, wiped the salt clear and left the table as the view outside of the booth returned to normal. The air seemed fresher. Jamie rested her head in her hands and sighed. "What else can go wrong?"

"Hi!" said a female voice.

Jamie jerked upright and cried out in alarm. The girl jumped back a step and also let out a yelp. As Jamie's heart raced, she realized it was the girl from the day before. "Parker, right?"

"Yes," Parker squeaked. Today, she wore a concert T-shirt for Broken Gazebo and had decorated her eye shadow with leopard spots. "Sorry, didn't mean to startle you."

"No it's fine." Jamie hesitated, her face growing warm. Had Parker really been asking her out on a date? "Was there something you wanted?"

Parker froze for a moment. Finally, something clicked and she said, "Yes. Yes, there is. Mind if I sit down?"

Jamie shrugged, trying to look casual though she felt anxiety creeping in for no good reason. "Be my guest."

"So…" Parker drummed her fingers on the table.

"So." Jamie nodded, then mentally kicked herself for being such a dork.

"Right, so I didn't get an answer yesterday about roller derby tomorrow. We got interrupted. I spotted you here when that creeper you were with got up to go, so I figured I'd see if you'd decided." Parker flashed a grimace of a smile.

A spirit cat jumped up onto the table and began grooming itself. Jamie fought the urge to swat it away.

"Oh yeah. Derby. Why is it you want to take me to roller derby? I think that was my huge sticking point. Is this like a date or something? I never get invited anywhere so this is a little out of the blue. And since yesterday, I've gotten a bit more paranoid." Jamie stopped abruptly, realizing she'd been rambling.

"Well…" Parker paused with her mouth open. "Yes. This is kind of a date. Or, I mean, I'm hoping it's a date. Assuming I've read you right and you like girls. I've seen you around school and I thought you always seemed interesting and like someone I'd like to… get to know better. And Steven Carmichael used to give me purple nurples when I was eight, so seeing him get his ass kicked is a huge plus for me." Parker used her hands to form a heart in front of her chest. In a quieter voice she added, "And, you know, you're smokin' hot."

The last statement caught Jamie as she took a sip of her mocha, and she choked.

Parker hesitated. "Too aggressive? You can tell me to stop any time. I've stopped tackling girls I like, so I figure that's an improvement."

Jamie shook her head. "Just… surprising. I don't get hit on very often, and never by a girl."

Parker bared her teeth in a smile again. Her manic energy struck Jamie as adorable in a way. But Jamie didn't know what to say, and so they sat in silence until Parker began to relax her smile and rub her cheeks.

"Okay, so that's starting to hurt." She looked back at Jamie and said, "My gaydar led me astray, didn't it? You're not gay."

Jamie opened her mouth, but the words didn't come. She didn't know how to answer. Relationships were something that people without a secret identity had. But she did find the thought of spending an evening with Parker appealing.

Slowly Jamie said, "I'm not saying that…" Parker perked up in response. "But I just don't have time to see anyone. I… I'm just really busy with… stuff."

"Oh." Parker frowned. "Okay. I'm… really sorry that I chased after you so much."

Parker started to slide out of the booth, but Jamie found herself saying, "Wait."

The other girl looked over expectantly.

Jamie racked her brain for something that could explain why she wanted Parker to stay. "Um, uh… What do you know about 2thefairest?"

"The gossip blog?" Parker shrugged, looking confused. "I've read it a few times. It's got some juicy stuff on there. Half the school wants to hug her, the other half want to murder her."

"You think it's a girl?" Jamie asked.

Parker chuckled. "Have you met the boys at our school? I can't imagine any of them have the brain power to write that well, let alone keep track of that kind of dirt. I'd bet money this is a girl. Why?"

"I'm trying to find out who's behind it," Jamie said. "Since they set me up for the showdown with Carmichael. If you can help me do that, I will go with you anywhere that you want."

Parker smiled "*Quid pro quo*, huh?"

"What's that?"

"I don't know. I got it from *Silence of the Lambs*."

Jamie shook her head and smiled. "I don't know what to make of you."

"Oh, I'm sure you say that to all the girls. So anywhere, huh?" Parker asked, a goofy smile on her face. "I can come up with a lot of anywheres." Jamie felt herself blushing again. "And I can appreciate payback. Revenge runs in my family. I don't know who's behind the blog, but I know the perfect person to help us find out. She's a computer expert. But she's not here right now, so I'm going to have to introduce you to Glenda first."

~

Glenda turned out to be Parker's 1976 Buick Regal two-door, filled with dirty laundry, fast food wrappers, and roller derby programs. The street it sat on looked half flooded, leaves clogging the storm drains, leaving icy pools of water on the edges. Jamie waited while Parker shoveled everything into her back seat. "It's not normally this bad," Parker said with a nervous smile.

"It's usually worse," a woman's voice said from inside the car. "But she always cleans up a bit when she's going courting."

Jamie tilted her head down to see a woman in her forties with a Farrah-Fawcett-style feathered hairdo in the back seat: Glenda, the spirit of the Buick. She wore a crop top and high-waisted jeans. Jamie gave a small wave to the spirit right before she heard a loud riot of banging metal nearby.

Parker and Jamie both looked over in time to see a half-dozen brushed-steel robot giraffes round the corner and gallop down the street past them. Chunks of asphalt tore up under their metal hooves as they ran. Dragging behind the last giraffe was a man wearing riot gear and a helmet that concealed his face. He held on to a nylon rope connected to a grappling hook attached to the giraffe's back. As his giraffe rounded the corner, he swung out wide and collided with trash cans across the street before the giraffe dragged him through one of the small lakes in the street and continued down the road. The spirit of the street, its skin asphalt black, ran in circles and cried in terror.

"Who the hell was that?" Parker asked, holding a handful of clothing as she watched the giraffes continue down the street.

"The Traffic Enforcer," Jamie said. "He normally beats up people who talk on their cell phone while driving or who don't know how to deal with roundabouts. I'm surprised he's dealing with something that big."

"Well, guess I need to get serious about a hands-free device. How about those giraffes? Tik-Tok?"

"From Technocracy Incorporated?" Jamie asked. "Yeah, seems most likely."

"Well, good to see insane robot-building terrorists are still getting work," Parker said. She dumped the clothing into the back seat, and a shiny scrap caught Jamie's attention.

"Are those panties?" Jamie asked, stunned that someone would keep underwear in the front seat of her car.

Parker paused with one in her hand. "What these? No, these are my derby shorts. I have, like, a million of these." She held them up to show that they said "Game Over" across the back of them. In a smarmy salesman voice she said, "I'm not just a fan, I'm also a junior derby player." She tossed the shorts to Jamie and walked around to the other side of the car. "Let's boogie."

Jamie tossed the shorts into the back seat and hopped in.

"In the category of 'going anywhere with me' can I talk you into dinner tomorrow? I'm thinking someplace classy, like Friendly's. Before you say anything, this is also my treat."

Jamie frowned at Parker. "Really? Is your friend so awesome that you need to splurge on me?"

"Friend's a strong word. I've come to think of her as someone I've met. But no. I'm doing this because I really want to spend an evening with you and introduce you to the wonders of roller derby."

"You're really big on the roller derby."

"It's like a cult. Except not creepy."

Jamie looked in the back seat at the spirit. "Glenda? Can I trust her?"

Glenda shrugged. "Yeah. She's a good kid. Lousy at car maintenance, but well intentioned."

"Ha, ha," Parker said, not privy to Glenda's side of the conversation. She looked confused, but willing to play along. "Very funny. I'm sure my car will tell you I'm very sweet and safe to be around."

Jamie winked at Parker. Jamie didn't let people in on her powers, but found that she could get away with using them when people thought she was just goofing around. No one believed you had a superpower if you weren't wearing a cape and cowl. "No ulterior motives or anything?"

"Do you think I'd tell you if she did? I'm her car, y'know. Though I guess you know she wants to get in your pants, right?"

Jamie didn't have an answer to that. "Anything else I should know?"

"Yeah, tell her I'm due for an oil change. Getting stiff and messy down there, y'know? Next thing you know my engine seizes and it's a one-way trip to the scrapyard for me."

"I'll pass it along." Jamie said and turned to Parker. "She says she needs an oil change."

"Um, thanks," Parker said with a frown. "You're... you're just joking about the oil change, right?"

"No." Jamie hesitated, then gave a conspiratorial wink. "I, uh, saw one of those window stickers in your back seat."

Parker, smiling with understanding, dropped the subject. As she tore away from the curb with the sound of screeching tires, she said, "So, about dinner..."

~

Parker and Jamie stood in front of a two-story house in one of the nicer parts of Karlsburg, white with pale blue trim. Ivy grew up a lattice beside the house and a low hedge ran along the winding path up to the house. The old woman in the house next door watched them from her window.

Jamie usually avoided this part of Karlsburg. In this section of the neighborhood, the immigrant vibe was more German, Irish, and Italian than Indian, Hispanic, and Arabic. She always got funny looks when she came around here, and Parker's haphazard parking job didn't help. Even coming up the walk to the door, all of the gnomish lawn spirits up and down the street watched them with suspicion, leaving Jamie with the feeling that the snooping wasn't just contained to one neighbor.

"Really?" Jamie asked as Parker led the way to the front door. "Your computer expert is here?"

Parker shrugged. "Well, yeah. What were you expecting?"

"An underground coffee shop made out of an abandoned video game arcade?"

"Nah, that's over in Quayside and the boy-stank in there will drop a moose. I'm hoping Ashley is home so that we don't have to go over there."

"Email won't do?"

"People can ignore email." Parker flashed a smile and added, "I'm much harder to ignore."

Parker rang the doorbell and danced in place while she waited for someone to answer. Jamie smiled at Parker's goofing around until she noticed the neighbor had come out and begun watering the lawn. She wore a wide-brimmed sun-hat that hid her eyes. Jamie could tell by body language that the woman was looking in their direction. She waved at the woman, who jerked in surprise and turned to look at the ground.

Jamie sighed.

The door opened and stopped when the chain hit the end of its reach. Jamie saw little of the face that peeked through the door besides glasses, acne, and blonde hair. A pendant necklace with a bunch of arrows pointing out from a central point glinted in the light. The person looked back and forth between Parker and Jamie.

"Can I help you?" The voice was definitely a girl.

Parker led the charge. "Hi Ashley! I'm Parker and this is—"

"I know who you are. What do you want?"

"Jamie here is trying to figure out who is behind the 2thefairest blog. I figured you're really good with computers and you've gotten trashed on the blog as well. So you would be the awesomest person to try and catch this blogger."

Ashley stared at them without responding right away. Finally, "You know you're not supposed to feed trolls, right?"

"Huh?" Parker asked. "Oh, you mean like internet trolls!"

41

Ashley closed her eyes. "Yes. Like internet trolls."

"So… that's a no?" Parker asked, anxiety creeping into her voice.

"I don't want to give this person more power than they have already. I'd rather ignore this person and let them move on to someone else."

Parker leaned in closer, blocking Jamie's view of Ashley. "Ashley, I don't think you understand. I get to have dinner and roller derby with Jamie if you'll help. Pleeeeeease?"

"I'll think about it, but I'm very busy with school." Ashley closed the door.

"Thank you, thank you, thank you!" Parker squealed as she jumped up and down. "I'll see you Monday!"

"Well, that was a dead end," Jamie said as they walked back towards the sidewalk.

"Does this mean you're not up for derby if I can't pull this off?"

Jamie hadn't thought about that. She'd gotten used to the idea of going out with Parker, and hadn't thought of the possibility that this could fall apart on her.

When Jamie didn't answer right away, Parker filled the silence. "I could, like, owe you for derby. And there are cookies. I'll totally buy you cookies at the bout!"

"Cookies, huh?" They had reached Glenda and stood on the sidewalk. "How can a girl turn down cookies?"

Parker began jumping up and down, shaking her fists and yelling, "Woo hoo!" Jamie laughed and shook her head, turning towards Glenda in time to see a police car roll up.

The policeman rolled down the passenger-side window and looked at Glenda parked diagonally across the sidewalk. "Have you been… parked here long?"

"Just a few minutes, officer," Parker said, regaining composure abruptly. "Just leaving."

"Have you kids seen anyone suspicious sneaking around?"

"Sorry, officer," Jamie said, fighting off the urge to turn and look back at Ashley's neighbor. "Just us kids."

CHAPTER 6 - MAJOR TOMBOY

Jamie never thought she'd be fussing over her clothes on a Friday night, but there she stood scrutinizing her outfit in the mirror. Of course, she imagined most girls weren't figuring out where to hide weapons. She didn't normally worry about this, but life had been weird and tonight was way outside her comfort zone. She had chosen her baggiest sweatshirt and jeans, but realized that she couldn't hide much if she got too warm and had to take off her coat.

At first, Jamie thought she'd be in too much trouble to go out to roller derby with Parker, but her mom hadn't grounded her after banishing her. Jamie had asked about roller derby over dinner the night before and at first Gloria just looked surprised. But when she finally spoke she said it was fine and added, "It's nice to see you still have friends."

Jamie turned to see if she could spot any suspicious bulges, but couldn't make out either the butterfly knife she'd duct taped to one calf or the folding knife she'd taped to her other. Jamie's mom couldn't understand at the time why Jamie could possibly want Hello Kitty duct tape. To Jamie, the very existence of Hello Kitty duct tape required it to be bought. Now, she didn't think she could explain to her mom the use she'd found.

She would have just put the knives in her pocket, but didn't know if she'd be searched at the bout. She hated leaving the neighborhood because she didn't have established relationships with the other neighborhood spirits. But then, Karl had continued to be silent. She'd snuck out while her mom was at work and tried to make contact with him, but nothing worked.

Karl had been the first spirit to approach her when her powers first manifested, back when Jamie thought she'd been losing her mind. She was twelve years old, her grandfather had just died, and she saw death and suffering in every alley she passed. Karl's influence had been part of what had made her decide to become a crime fighter despite her mother's persistent hatred of their existence. She also relied on him for all of her legwork. She'd be spending the weekend reading the *Gazette* online, trying to learn more about the missing students.

"Jamie!" her mom called from downstairs. "Your friend Parker is here!"

Jamie hesitated, then grabbed her brass knuckles and stuffed them into one pocket. She got to the door and then ran back to grab her wrist *onenju* and slip it on before running down the stairs. She didn't know if holy symbols besides crosses would work if she ran into that vampire again, but it was worth a shot. She nearly tripped and fell when she saw the smile on her mom's face. Gloria looked relaxed and genuinely happy. Jamie hadn't seen her mom like that since before Grandpa Brown's death. "Are you okay, Mom?"

"Just fine, sweetie." Gloria's face looked like it might crack from the size of the smile on her face. "Your friend was just explaining roller derby. It sounds like a lot of fun. I really hope you guys enjoy it."

"Hi, Jamie," Parker said. She'd styled her hair up into a fauxhawk and was wearing what looked like a sports jersey. On the front, a creepy doll in roller skates stood above the printed words "Glass-Eyed Roller Dolls."

Parker spread her arms when Jamie came down the stairs, but Jamie just waved back distractedly and stared at her mother

Jamie's dad poked his head out of his office. "Have fun, girls!"

"It was nice to meet you, Mrs. Hattori," Parker said, heading for the door. "Hi, Mr. Hattori!" Jamie stumbled as she moved to follow Parker. As Parker pulled on her coat, Jamie noticed "Major Tomboy" printed on the back of the jersey, with the number "4321" underneath it.

"Jamie?" Gloria called.

Jamie turned and looked back expectantly.

"Don't I at least get a hug before you leave?"

Beating up muggers had left Jamie on guard most of the time, and even before that she hadn't been a very huggy person. But Jamie hadn't seen her mom this happy in years and didn't want to jinx it. She walked back, hugged her mom stiffly, and followed Parker out.

Outside, the first thing Jamie could think to say was, "Who are you and what did you do with my real mom?"

All Parker could say was, "Huh?"

Jamie realized how bizarre that must sound. "Sorry, my mom has been angry at me for no reason for years. Seeing her smiling is nice but... creepy."

"Well, I'm glad I can bring joy into your life," Parker said as she unlocked the passenger side door for Jamie. She held it open while Jamie got in, closed the door and then went over to the other side.

As they pulled away from the curb, Jamie said, "I guess she's happy to see I have a social life of some sort."

"I guess that would explain why I don't see much of you outside of school."

Jamie shrugged. "I just don't have time for people."

"Out all night wearing a mask and beating up bad guys?" Parker laughed at her own joke.

Jamie tensed. She wondered if she could discreetly search Parker's car for apples. "No. I, uh, volunteer a lot at my church."

"I... I didn't know you were religious."

"I've sort of drifted away from attending service, but I help out after school. Filing. Cleaning. Helping move the Buddha around."

"Um, Buddha? I thought those were called temples."

"Sorry, I guess it's weird from the outside. It's a tradition from Japan, which got Americanized when they got here. So we have a minister, pews, sing songs on Sundays. And a big golden Buddha at the front of the church."

"I could see that being awkward." Parker laughed. "Maybe I can get you to take me to church with you."

Jamie shrugged. "I don't go to service much anymore, but I guess I could take me to church with you."

"Eeeeeexcellent."

"So, what's Major Tomboy?" Jamie asked.

"That's my derby name. Almost everyone in derby has one."

"How'd you get that one?"

Parker smiled. "I chose it. I wanted something sort of glam and spacy. Like Ziggy Stardust-ish. 'Jammer from Mars' seemed kinda clunky. There was already a ref named Major Tom, so I figured this would be a good alternative. Though my number is *technically* from Peter Schilling's song. I figure using 'tomboy' emphasizes my butch side."

"Butch, huh?"

"Yup." She turned and bared her teeth at Jamie. "Grrr!"

"Do you have to wear your jersey to every derby thing? Is this part of the cult?"

Parker laughed. "Nah. We're just doing a raffle tonight to raise money for travel games, so I'm expected to be in uniform. Hopefully you don't mind me running around and shilling tickets once in a while, do you?"

"I think I can survive by myself for a little bit."

"Great, I'd hate for you to get into another fight without me." Parker picked up her MP3 player and began flipping through songs. "So what kind of music do you listen to?"

"J-pop," Jamie said. "But I can listen to whatever."

Pizzicato Five's "Twiggy Twiggy" began to play from the speakers. "Your wish is my command. So, do you think Kyo or Yuki is the best guy for Tohru?"

"Huh? Oh, wait, you mean in *Fruits Basket?*" She burst out laughing. She hadn't had this sort of conversation since Dharma School. "I'm totally Team Kyo. So you like *anime?*"

"I can neither confirm nor deny that I own a pair of cat ears. But if I did, I'd look very *kawaii* in them." Parker beamed. "I think we're going to get along."

~

Jamie and Parker clutched each other, screaming in excitement as Stiletto Libretto from the team Last Laff tried to make another scoring pass. Cleopatra Thunder, from the Disco Valkyries, tried to stop her but Stiletto's teammates, Vladi Impaler and Heidi Your Boyfriend ran interference. Stiletto squeaked through and called off the jam.

Jamie, heart pounding, sat back down in the bleachers and shared an excited smile with Parker. Jamie couldn't decide if she liked roller derby, but she definitely loved it. She didn't understand all the rules, and the idea of roller skating didn't excite her, but there was something about the energy of the sport and the players that sucked her in.

Jamie had competed in many sports when she was little: kendo, karate, kyudo, tae kwon do, judo, aikido, and gymnastics. In all those sports but gymnastics, not many girls competed. And each of those sports had been solitary affairs. There were teams, but her success or failure was entirely dependent on individual performance. Derby was very much a team event, and one entirely made up of women to boot.

While waiting for the next jam to start, the skaters chatted or danced around to the music the DJ played through the gymnasium. Throughout the game, Jamie had marveled that the players could be so friendly between jams and so ruthless while playing.

A whistle blew, and the pack of skaters began moving. Pacing the skaters were the spirits for the teams: a shieldmaiden in gold lamé armor with a blonde afro stuck near the Disco Valkyries, while a cadaverous woman in clown makeup followed Last Laff. All of the spirits for the team, including the zombie clown and the tusked matron of the league as a whole, were beautiful and female. Even the spirit of the referee team was female, despite most of the officials being male. The message was clear to Jamie: men might come in here, but this was a place for women.

The man on the bench next to her, who had introduced himself as Marcus, nudged Jamie during a lull in the action. "Do you know her?"

Jamie followed the line of Marcus's gaze. She saw a dark-skinned girl, wearing a shirt like Parker's, glaring in Jamie's general direction.

"No clue who she is," Jamie said. "Are you sure she's even looking at me?"

"Rachel thinks she is," Marcus said, indicating the tattooed friend he sat next to. "She's usually got a good eye for these sorts of things."

Jamie shrugged, trying to keep her freak out instinct in check. "I'll keep my eyes peeled."

The clock hit the end of the first half. People began standing and exiting the bleachers. Parker tugged on Jamie's arm.

"C'mon. I want some popcorn." Parker walked down the steps and slid her hand down to Jamie's to pull her along. "If you play your cards right, I might even buy you a T-shirt."

Jamie didn't really want popcorn or a T-shirt, but she was reluctant to pull out of Parker's grip. She wasn't sure about the "date" aspect of this excursion, but she definitely enjoyed the feel of Parker's hand in her own. With a laugh, she stood and followed.

According to Parker, one of the four home teams sat out each bout to do all the vending and other volunteer work while another home team played a visiting team. The super-hero themed Excessive Force were playing the visiting team in the second match of the night while Lafayette's Lightning Brigade stood behind merchandise tables in the lobby wearing their blue and silver uniforms and miniature tricorn hats.

In the middle of the lobby, three girls moved to intercept Jamie and Parker. The girl from across the gym, who seemed to be leading the charge, stepped forward. She was flanked by two other girls wearing Glass-Eyed Dolls jerseys.

"This your new girlfriend, Tom?" the girl asked.

"Hey, Crass," Parker said. "Was there something you wanted or were you hoping to just crap on my evening?"

Crass looked like she was spoiling for a fight, but Jamie could tell right away she'd be able to take the other girl and her two friends. She just didn't know what the deal was. Junior roller derby politics? Out of the corner of her eye, Jamie noticed Marcus and Rachel. They looked like they were just chatting about the T-shirts, but their body language indicated they were watching Jamie. This did not help Jamie's sense of paranoia.

"Look, I'm not the person who broke things off," Crass said. "Is this what it was all about? Some other dark meat that you want to get a taste of?"

"Slow down there," Jamie said. "I'm guessing you're the ex. Look, this isn't any of your business. Please unbind your panties."

"Hey, guys," Parker said, her voice turning shrill. "How about we all calm down? Jamie, this is my ex-girlfriend: Crass Hopper. Or Cassie if you don't like derby names. Crass, this is Jamie."

"So, what? Is Parker not good enough for you?" Crass demanded. "Because if she's not I can prove you wrong. With fists and stuff."

"Is there any right answer for you?" Jamie asked, exasperated. Rachel now stared directly at Crass, frowning. "Or are you just going to throw things at me until you find the justification to throw the first punch?"

"What, you think you can take me?" Crass asked.

Like a storm rolling into a valley, Cleopatra Thunder skated between Jamie and Crass and forced the two girls to take a step farther apart. Jamie smelled wet soil and ozone in the air. "Is there a problem here, girls?"

Cleopatra was not only one of the few black skaters out on the track, but also the only one with long dreads. Those two details made her someone Jamie was not likely to forget. Up close, Jamie saw that Cleopatra wore thick layers of makeup, probably to make it visible from the stands.

Crass looked down and mumbled, "No, ma'am."

Cleopatra turned to Jamie, who answered, "Nope. No problem."

"Okay, well, how about all of you going your separate ways, since there's no problem here."

After Crass had gotten far enough away, Cleopatra looked at Parker, shook her head and said, "I told you not to crap where you eat." Before Parker could reply, Cleopatra skated away.

Parker looked at Jamie. "So, um… Popcorn?"

~

Neither spoke in the car until Parker reached the West Key Bridge to get back to Karlsburg. Neither of them talked about the encounter with Crass during the bout, and conversation just died. Not even Glenda had anything to say. Instead, Jamie just stared out the passenger side window. As rough as Karlsburg was, the spirits of West Key looked more abused.

"So. I'm sorry about the whole Crass thing," Parker said, breaking the silence. "I don't know what was up with her."

"Yeah. For my first date of any sort, it could have been better." Jamie had meant to say it as a joke, but felt sad nonetheless.

Parker gaped at Jamie. "This could not have been your first date ever."

Jamie shrugged. "I don't have time for people."

"But seriously. Crass isn't usually like that. I don't know what happened."

"Apparently me."

After a few moments Parker said, "Seriously? First date ever?

Like ever ever?"

Jamie shrugged. "There are just a lot of things that need doing, and I only have so much time."

"Now who's hiding a secret about themselves?" Glenda asked from the backseat. Jamie didn't respond.

Parker stopped the car in front of Jamie's house. "Home again, home again," Parker whispered.

"Thank you," Jamie said, fumbling around for what to say. "I really did have fun tonight, all things considered."

"I'm glad." Parker hesitated then awkwardly patted Jamie on the arm.

"I'll see you Monday then?"

"Definitely."

Jamie smiled and got out of the car and stumbled on the curb. She waved goodbye to Parker, who waved back. They watched each other as Parker pulled away from the curb and drove into the night. Jamie didn't walk to her door till Glenda was out of sight.

CHAPTER 7 - IN CROWD AND OUT CROWD

People stared at Jamie as she walked down the school halls Monday morning, but gave her a wide berth. She didn't know how she felt about being feared. She dropped her backpack between her feet and began opening her locker.

"Jamie?" said a familiar voice behind her. She turned and saw a short, dumpy girl with dirty blonde hair, acne, and glasses. She wore a loose-fitting black T-shirt for "PAX EAST," jeans, and Chuck Taylors.

"If you're here to either invite me to roller derby or punch me, I'm going to say 'no' to both."

"No… I'm Ashley. You came by my house last Thursday wanting help finding out about that blog."

"Ooooh." Jamie finally recognized the sliver of face she'd seen through the door. "So did you find anything out? Some evil hacker or something?"

Ashley shook her head. "You don't need to be a technical genius to write a blog. I tried tracking down the domain name and the hosting service but that just hit dead ends. But I spent some time analyzing the gossip and the possible people who could have been behind it."

Jamie felt her heartbeat quicken. She could wrap up one of her problems in no time. "Yeah, so do you have a list or something?"

"Just one name so far, but I should probably wait until I have more information. I just wanted to let you, and Parker if I see her, know that I've made some progress."

This was unbelievable. Jamie couldn't just let this opportunity slip through her fingers. "Tell me what you got. This is driving me crazy."

Ashley pursed her lips and hesitated before whispering, "Sabrina Alvarez."

A switch flipped in Jamie's head and the rage exploded within her. She couldn't remember the last time she had been this mad. She scanned the area until she spotted the cheer captain down the hall, in her stupid cheer uniform. Other cheerleaders and some boys in letterman jackets hovered around her as she chatted with them. Jamie stalked down the hallway and people ran to get out of her way. Sabrina and her entourage noticed Jamie approaching long before Jamie got there. A few of the boys moved forward but Sabrina made eye contact with Jamie and herded them out of the way.

"Did you want something, kung fu girl?" Sabrina asked, arms folded across her chest.

Jamie didn't like that this was the one person who wasn't afraid of her. "I think you've been spreading rumors about me." Her muscles relaxed into fighting stance, and her harsh breathing was loud in her ears.

"I wouldn't consider them rumors," Sabrina said with a sneer and an arched eyebrow. "I told people your dreads weren't real, but that's just my opinion."

Jabbing a finger in Sabrina's direction, Jamie said, "No, you're the blogger that's writing as 2thefairest."

Sabrina huffed in annoyance. "Like I have the time to repeat everyone's trash talk on the Internet. Why don't you run off before you get yourself suspended again?"

The other cheerleaders tittered, then stopped as Jamie looked at them. Jamie clenched her fists and took a deep breath, planning on really laying into that bitch of a cheerleader when a man's voice said, "Miss Hattori, Miss Alvarez, is everything alright?"

Jamie turned to see Principal Mueller standing there, looking both determined and anxious at the same time. Fear of getting into more trouble with school and her mom cooled the fires of Jamie's rage. She tried to form words but they slipped away from her.

"Yes, Principal Mueller," Sabrina said. "I was just giving Jamie a bit of good-natured teasing about her suspension, and I accidentally pushed her too far. Isn't that right, Jamie? I was just about to apologize when you came up." Sabrina extended her hand towards Jamie. "I'm awfully sorry I razzed you so hard. No hard feelings?"

Jamie grabbed Sabrina's hand and squeezed, but found that Sabrina had quite the grip of her own. "No hard feelings."

"Well, good to see you know how to solve problems without your fists, Miss Hattori."

Jamie didn't say anything further as she slouched back to finish putting her bag in her locker. After her rage, she felt burnt out and empty.

~

At lunch, Jamie swung by the trophy case. While she had been suspended, the school had posted photos of the missing students. A few students stared in mute terror at the faces of the missing kids; others seemed to have gotten used to them and went about their day. Jamie wondered, not for the first time, if people in Cobalt City had just gotten used to awful things happening to people.

The pictures on the glass case represented the fringes of the school culture: the druggies, the nerds, the emos, and the plain old losers. Had someone declared war on the weirdos of Lincoln High? And since she was so anti-social, was she going to be on this hit list?

One face stood out for Jamie: the vampire she had fought the week before was one of the missing students. Connor Laird, a junior at the school. She'd seen his name in the *Gazette*, but hadn't connected it until she saw the photo. She took a step back to look at the other pictures. Was this what happened to the other missing kids? Had they all become vampires like Connor?

"I don't know why people are so bent out of shape," Sabrina said. Jamie jerked in surprise and turned to face the cheerleader, who stood there without her usual entourage. "It's just the losers who are missing, like anyone cares. I'm sure they're just off writing fake suicide notes and pretending to be wizards in tunnels or something."

Jamie clenched her fists, not daring to speak. Instead, she mentally recited the *nembutsu*.

"Oh, what?" Sabrina asked. "Still think I'm behind the blog? Or is this just general hatred of the cool kids?"

A cry of pain, the clatter of plastic, and laughter interrupted Jamie's retort. She turned to see Ashley sprawled out on the ground, her cafeteria tray upended and her food scattered all over the floor.

"Uh oh," Sabrina said with a laugh. "Nerd down."

"Guess you should be more careful!" one boy called out, prompting more people to laugh.

Jamie walked over and stood next to Ashley. To the assembled crowd, she said, "If you aren't going to help clean this up, I suggest you move along."

The crowd looked away and dispersed. Jamie didn't like being feared, but didn't mind the fringe benefits. She knelt down to Ashley and helped her stand up. Food covered the other girl's shirt and face.

"You shouldn't have done that," Ashley whispered. "It will just be worse next time."

"Should I just leave you standing here with shepherd's pie on your face then? Or do you want me to help you clean it off in the restroom?"

Ashley looked down at herself. "I guess I won't say no to help."

As Jamie walked Ashley to the restroom, she wondered if Ashley could be the next disappearance. An idea began to form in Jamie's head, but she'd need Parker's help. Jamie asked, "Say, Ashley, have you ever been on a stakeout?"

~

Parker slouched down in Glenda's driver's seat and groaned. "I'm feeling a little used."

Jamie patted Parker on the arm while watching Sabrina walk back out to her car. The cheerleader had changed out of her cheer uniform and wore jeans and a T-shirt instead. Jamie had always expected Sabrina would drive a candy-apple red convertible of some sort, and not a wood-paneled Ford station wagon that looked old enough to be Sabrina's father. Jamie couldn't understand why.

"What happened to you owing me? Squid pro mow and all?"

From the back of the car Ashley said, "Do you mean *quid pro quo*?"

"Were you born without a sense of humor, Ashley?" Parker

asked. To Jamie she said, "That's the only reason I'm doing this. That and your pretty smile."

Jamie swallowed hard and looked back towards Sabrina. "Here she goes," she said. Her voice cracked and she cleared her throat. "If it makes you feel better, I don't enjoy this either. Patience isn't my strong suit."

Parker pulled away from the curb and followed Sabrina as she continued driving around on her evening errands.

Ashley asked, "If she's the blogger, what are you hoping to catch while following her?"

Jamie hesitated, not wanting to admit this was all a ploy to keep an eye on Ashley. And she didn't think she knew the other girls well enough to suggest that Sabrina was an apple-wielding magical super-villain.

"There's just so much weird stuff going on," Jamie said. "She's so… awful I can only imagine she's got more than just this blog on her plate."

"That's quite a reach," Parker said. "Lucky for you I'm a sucker for a pretty face."

Parker's comment triggered an automatic smile from Jamie, who looked away in embarrassment.

Ashley sighed. "If you need me to watch for something, let me know. Otherwise, I'm going to work on homework."

"Actually," Jamie said. "I have a question. Ashley, do you know what *Oriental Adventures* are?"

Ashley frowned in confusion. "Like in *Dungeons & Dragons*?"

Jamie shrugged. "Dunno. All I know is those two words."

"It's the name of a rule book for *Dungeons & Dragons*. One version came out in 1985, the other in 2001. It provided rules for playing Asian themed characters instead of European. So it had monks, samurai, ninjas, yakuza… kensei."

"Okay. That helps a lot." Jamie thought she'd detected a pause before the word "kensei," but couldn't decide if she was being too paranoid.

Ashley scowled and returned to her homework. Jamie had noticed that Glenda's spirit hadn't put in an appearance on this car trip. Spirits did sometimes just lay low, but Jamie missed having her in the back seat. She wondered if Glenda just didn't like sharing the back with someone else.

Parker stopped the car again. Jamie watched Sabrina go into a vitamin store while Parker did something with her cell phone. After the cheerleader disappeared into the store, Parker angled her cell phone so Jamie could see the screen. Parker had written a text message that said, "y did u bring ash?"

Jamie took the phone from Parker and typed in, "worried that she might be next missing kid."

"is that ur job?"

Jamie stared at those words, trying to figure out a reasonable answer while maintaining her secret identity. Finally she typed, "if not me who?"

Parker rolled her eyes and looked back towards the store.

"You know, if you want to talk in private I can just go home," Ashley said.

"Don't worry, Ashley," Parker said, drumming her fingers on the steering wheel. "That should be the end of secret messages for today. Jamie shot down my request to suck face later so I'm just going to sulk in my rejection."

Jamie coughed in surprise and looked back and forth between Parker and Ashley. Parker grinned impishly and waggled her eyebrows while Ashley turned bright red and hid behind a calculus text book. Jamie's own cheeks felt warm, but she hoped no one could tell she was blushing.

"Speaking of changing the subject," Jamie said, louder than intended. "Here comes Sabrina."

The cheerleader walked back towards her car, holding a four-pack of Muscle Milk. She hesitated halfway there before turning and walking towards Glenda.

"Oh, poop," said Parker.

Sabrina walked up to the driver-side window and knocked. Parker cranked down the window.

"Can I help you three with something?" Sabrina asked.

"I'd like the bacon cheeseburger combo," Parker said. "No onions, extra pickles, and a strawberry shake for the drink. Anybody else know what they want?"

Sabrina huffed. "Very funny, lesbo. I've seen you following me for the last hour."

"Lesbo? Is that really the best you can come up with?" Parker asked. "Who even uses that word?"

"Whatever." Sabrina leaned down to look across the car at Jamie. "You know, Jamie, if I was really your blogger you probably wouldn't catch me in the act while I'm at Karlsburg Vitamins. Just sayin'."

"Thanks for the tip," Jamie said. She wouldn't be doing another stakeout like this again. She'd have to figure out some other way to keep Ashley out of trouble.

Sabrina straightened and headed back to her car. "Oh, and be careful who you hang out with. I hear 'dyke' and 'loser' are contagious."

Parker cranked up her window. "Well, I guess this means the stakeout is over. I vote for a nutritious dinner at Don Juan's Tacos. I need me some nachos and Jarritos right now."

"Sure," Jamie said. "Let me call my mom and let her know I won't be home for dinner."

"I really should get home," Ashley said. "With all the disappearances my parents worry a lot."

"Alright, I can make a detour to your place." Parker tore out of her parking spot with the squeal of tires on pavement. Another driver honked at her as she careened down the street. "Hey, Jamie, you doing anything tomorrow night?"

Jamie paused on the verge of calling her mom. "Um, just the usual work. Why? I hope you don't want to try this again."

"Ha, no. I've had enough of Sabrina for this year. I have derby practice and I was wondering if you wanted to come by and hang out. You'd need to bus out to West Key but I could give you a ride home."

"Depends," Jamie said. "Am I going to have 'Crass Hopper' in my face again?"

Parker smiled. "Nah. If she gives you any trouble, I'll beat her up."

"Then sure. I may even get my mom to drive me. She really likes me spending time with you."

Parker smiled with smug satisfaction.

Ashley leaned forward in her seat. "Mind if I go too?"

When Parker hesitated, Jamie jumped in. "I think it would be great if both of us could go."

Parker sighed. "Sure. Sounds great."

"Awesome!" Ashley said with a smile. "I really like roller derby and it would be neat to see you guys practice."

Parker shrugged. "Yeah, it should be great."

Jamie hoped Ashley couldn't see the annoyed look on Parker's face.

CHAPTER 8 - MORE BLOODSUCKING OWLS

Under cover of night, Kensei crouched in the crook of the tree across from the Alvarez home and peered through the orange and yellow leaves. In her right hand, she held her *onenju* and thumbed through the beads while mentally chanting the *nembutsu*. In her ear, the chatter of police droned on. The neighborhood surprised Kensei as much as Sabrina's car. This was a poorer neighborhood than the one where Kensei's family lived. The spirits looked starved, unloved, frayed around the edges. The way Sabrina dressed, she didn't seem like she struggled. Kensei wondered how Sabrina got her money.

Kensei had left home just after dinner and arrived at seven, but an hour later there was still no sign of Sabrina. Instead, she got to watch the blue flickering light of the television wash over the faces of the Sabrina's parents and siblings as they watched one of the *Toy Story* movies.

Out of desperation, Kensei whispered, "Karl, are you around?"

"Yes, for a moment," Karl said from the branches of the tree next to her. The sound so startled Kensei that she nearly fell out of her tree.

"Where the hell have you been?" Kensei whispered.

"Investigating." Karl looked tired, as though he hadn't slept in days. "I am trying to determine the full extent of my numbness. It is very subtly done, and there have been many false leads. I have needed to cover every inch of the neighborhood and examine my senses from different angles. I believe the numbness is spreading slowly."

"What sort of person could do that?" Kensei asked.

"Anyone with magical abilities and time. It is clear that this has been something that has been building up for months."

"Could a god have done this?"

"Potentially. Why do you think that?"

"Malenfant approached me at Shambalah and told me he wanted me to deal with a god in the area."

"That is very troubling. I will add it to my list of things to investigate."

Instead of disappearing, he jumped down to the ground and began walking.

"Wait, Karl!" Kensei hissed.

Karl stopped and looked back up towards her.

"Do you know anything about a blog called 2thefairest?"

"No."

Kensei cursed. "Do you know if Sabrina is some sort of enemy?"

"At the moment, no. Her house is numb to me and I can only barely sense her when she leaves. Prior to this confusion, she was not an enemy of yours. I cannot speak for now."

"Do you at least know where she is right now?"

"She crossed the bridge from Lafayette Park about ten minutes ago and should be home in another ten minutes, barring misfortune. I believe she has a seasonal job in the park, but that is hard to tell. Lafayette Park is beyond my purview."

"Okay. What are you doing right now?"

"I was nearby because the Alvarez house has disappeared to me. I am examining the boundaries of this numbness."

Kensei frowned. Was Sabrina the god that Malenfant had mentioned? Was she hiding her presence? "Well, let me know if there's anything I can do to help."

"I believe it was you who pointed out that this is a problem I must solve, since you need sleep and homework. Should I need your help, I will let you know."

Kensei hated having her words thrown back at her, but said nothing. Without another word, Karl walked away down the sidewalk, his right hand stretched in the direction of the Alvarez house. He walked to the end of the block, hesitated, turned left and disappeared around the corner.

Like clockwork, Sabrina's station wagon pulled into the driveway ten minutes later. Kensei watched the cheerleader walk from her car and into the house. Inside, Sabrina poked her head into the living room before heading upstairs. Once upstairs, Sabrina's silhouette went through the motions of changing clothes and then sat at a table.

For the next hour Kensei watched Sabrina sit there. The masked hero couldn't tell if Sabrina was studying, blogging, or anything. All Kensei could do was stew in frustration at the ambiguity. Finally Sabrina stood up, walked away from the window and the light went out.

Kensei stretched her legs to restore feeling before jumping down from the tree and creeping across the street. The Alvarez's yard spirit, which looked like a gargoyle, growled at Kensei as soon as she crossed the property line.

"It's okay." She pulled out a bottle of milk and poured out some on the lawn for the gargoyle. "I can play nice."

The gargoyle crept forward and sniffed at the milk before going through the motions of lapping it up. Kensei turned to walk towards the house again and found a stern gray-haired Hispanic-looking spirit with long hair and a beard. Probably the house spirit. He wore simple brown robes.

"Your pagan tricks will not work here," the spirit said.

"Oh, man," Kensei whispered. "Please tell me you're not Jesus."

That seemed to annoy the spirit more. "I am José. What are you doing intruding here?"

"Are you the spirit of the house?"

"I am the protector."

Kensei fought the urge to roll her eyes over the quibbling. "I'm just here to ask you some questions."

"I doubt I have anything to say to you."

"Is Sabrina a magic-wielding blogger with a thing for apples?"

José opened his mouth to respond, then froze. "I'm sorry, what?" He shook his head. "No. Don't answer. I don't want to know and my answer is the same: I will not divulge anything about the family of the house."

"But what if Sabrina is hurting people? Do you really want her to keep doing that?"

"I can assure you, Sabrina is no enemy to you." He seemed

troubled by that statement.

Before Kensei could ask for clarification someone said from behind her, "You know talking to yourself is a sign of madness, Kensei."

Kensei spun around and saw her vampire from the week before, Connor, with two other teenagers. One of the newcomers was a painfully thin girl in black jeans, a black tank-top, and a fishnet long-sleeve shirt. Her hair looked intentionally messed up and her eyes and mouth were outlined in black. The other was a tall, stocky guy with black hair pulled back into a ponytail. He wore blue jeans, a t-shirt with three wolves howling at the moon, and a long black trenchcoat. In one hand, he held a European-style broadsword. Kensei remembered the kids from the photographs on the trophy case. Her name was Courtney, his was Shane. As she concentrated, she could sense that they were not human.

"You know," Kensei said. "I was going to call today a waste until you showed up."

"Oh? Why's that?" Connor asked.

"Because I really want to hit something and I've got a whole fistful of 'oriental adventures' just for you."

While Connor puzzled over that, Kensei charged the vampires and drew her katana. Connor scrambled back in fear, leaving Courtney and Shane to face the superhero. Kensei slashed upward towards Courtney, who raised her arms in defense. The blade cut deep across the vampire girl's forearms and flames erupted along the cut. Courtney screamed and fell down, flailing her arms in an attempt to put the fire out. Kensei continued the swing to bring the blade to point at Shane's face.

Shane swung his sword to beat the katana out of line. Kensei struck back and he parried. She caught a bit of movement in the corner of her eye and turned to the left just as Connor tried to tackle her. She raised her left hand with her *onenju* on it. Connor collided with the beads, stopped like he'd hit a brick wall, and screamed. Shane chose this moment to swing his sword at Kensei again. She dodged out of the way and left Connor to take the hit. The sword dug deep into his shoulder and he growled in frustration.

"You jackass!" Connor snarled as he clutched his face where the beads had touched him. No blood came from his shoulder wound. "I thought you knew how to use that thing!"

Porch lights came on at the Alvarez home. Kensei suspected that the police had been called at this point. Screaming tended to attract that sort of attention. But it could be a good twenty minutes before they responded in this part of Karlsburg.

Shane continued swinging at Kensei, and she continued to parry and slip in little attacks. The vampire's skin was pocked with little burn marks and he looked wide-eyed with terror, but he wasn't stopping. On the front porch, the Alvarez family had gathered to watch the fight. Sabrina stood in front of the rest. Kensei made brief eye contact with the cheerleader, then turned back to the fight.

Kensei got a better look at Shane's sword as they fought. The blade looked cheaply made, perhaps even mass produced. She decided to put that to the test. She lured him into needing to swing just outside of his comfortable reach. Just before he hit her, she sidestepped and used his own momentum to knock him off balance. He was stopped from falling by his sword point ramming into the ground.

Kensei swung at his blade with her own and broke it in half. She continued her motion forward while he stared at his broken sword. She punched up with the pommel of her sword into his face. He fell backwards onto the lawn, unconscious.

Behind her, she heard Connor grunt in surprise. She spun in time to see him wipe out on the lawn with Sabrina on top of him. She was barefoot, wearing just a white-ribbed tank top and plaid pajama pants. As best Kensei could tell, Connor was about to ambush her while she was distracted with Shane. Sabrina tackled him before he could do it.

Roaring in rage, Connor threw Sabrina off of him. She flew across the yard and landed with a thump. Kensei hoped Sabrina was alright, and hated herself for being worried. While the vampire struggled to get to his feet, Kensei ran at him and kicked him in the face as hard as she could. He went out like a light.

Kensei looked around the lawn and saw Courtney staggering to her feet. Just as she tried to catch the other girl, Courtney changed into an owl and flew off.

"You're welcome!" Sabrina yelled.

Kensei turned to see the other girl standing up, grass stains all over her tank top. She glared at Kensei. The hero wanted to thank Sabrina but all she did was stare. She didn't know what to make of

Sabrina's heroism. Finally, she just waved awkwardly and ran off into the night.

~

Jamie came up the stairs of the church, carrying her backpack. It was nearly midnight. The nightlife of Karlsburg still ran strong across the street, but the church was dark. Agyo appeared on the steps, his *vajra* club aimed at Jamie's face. "Hold it right there, kid. You're hot."

She sighed. "Don't tell me you're hitting on me too."

"What?" The spirit frowned in confusion as his brain worked to catch up. "Oh. No. No! I just, well… you've got some sort of magic thing in your backpack that's hoodooing you."

"Crap!" Jamie growled as she pulled off her bag and began digging through it. Hidden at the bottom was an apple with Greek letters carved into it. How long had it been there? She hadn't kept the one from the fight in the alley. Did she have it in her bag when she blew her top at Sabrina this morning?

"It looks like the spell's mostly faded," Agyo said, "but you really need to chuck that thing before you get its mojo inside the church."

Jamie dropped it and kicked it away. "I don't need to go in the church. I just needed to ask you about something."

"Is this about someone hitting on you? Relationship stuff is more Ungyo's thing. I can go get him if you want to talk about that."

"How is he going to give advice when he doesn't talk? Won't he let all the good energy out if he opens his mouth?"

"Well, yeah," Agyo admitted. "But he gives really meaningful looks and gestures. I can interpret what he'd want to say to you. Just the way he arches his eyebrows is amazing."

Jamie shook her head in bafflement. "What makes either of you qualified to give advice on relationships?"

"Well, Ungyo has a lot of knowledge about compassion, loving kindness, that sort of stuff. And we have a copy *If the Buddha Dated* in the library. It's got a lot of really great tips."

"No. No, no, no!" Jamie scrubbed her face with her hands. "I'm too tired for this! I just want to know what sort of vampire turns into an owl instead of a bat. I've got a bunch of them in the neighborhood now and I don't know what to do about them. Do you know anything about vampire owls? Or did your knowledge of mythology get replaced with *If the Buddha Dated*?!"

A couple walked by on the sidewalk and looked at Jamie as though she were crazy.

"Slow down there, kiddo." Agyo said. "You've got some hatred rolling off you, and that just ain't gonna cut it here. How about you take some deep breaths, recite the nembutsu and get that temper under control. Amida Buddha might let you into the Pure Land, but I have one job in this church and that's keeping bad vibes away. So cool your jets."

It took at least ten minutes of chanting *"Namu Amida Butsu"* before Jamie didn't feel like hitting something. At that point, Agyo said, "I've given your question some thought, and this sounds like a *strix*. In Ancient Greece and Rome, *strix* was the word for owls. It also referred to birds of ill omen that fed on human flesh and blood."

"Why'd it have to be Greek?" Jamie groaned. "I don't want this all to be connected to the blog!"

"Well, hold on there, kid. Romans had *strixes* as well. And the *strix* fed into the myth of the Romanian *strigoi*, which is very similar to the modern idea of vampires. *Strigoi* could change into all kinds of animals. Not just bats or wolves."

"Oh, so this could still just be regular old vampires? Just cooler than previously thought?"

"Maybe. I don't know much about real vampires. I just have a bunch of books on mythology."

"Any idea who would know?"

Agyo shrugged. "You know how some churches have all kinds of ancient lore about real life demons?"

"Yeah?"

"This ain't that kind of church. And no one in the *sangha* is hip to this as far as I can tell. I mean, Steve Kawate has been studying astrology but hasn't gotten anywhere. But really, who believes in that stuff? You could try the Tibetans. They have all sorts of magic rituals. A little Mahakala empowerment might solve your problem. Mahakala's supposed to protect you from enemies."

"Yeah, don't want to go down that road. I don't know what the empowerment would do with my power. I don't need any more supernatural weirdness."

"Right. Maybe you can go find a vampire hunter?"

"And just where do I find a vampire hunter? If there are any cool superhero bars, I don't know where they are and I'm too young to go into them."

"Have you tried the phone book? Like under 'V'? Or it could be 'H'. I imagine that you have to deal with all sorts of weird stuff if you're in that line of work. Not just vampires. Or maybe they're all grouped under Pest Control?"

"Great." Jamie felt defeated and wanted to get home. "I'll try that out."

CHAPTER 9 - MORE APPLES

The next morning, as Jamie walked to her locker, she spotted Sabrina walking in her direction. The cheerleader stopped in front of her locker, a few down from Jamie, and began turning the dial of the combination lock. Sabrina looked tired but otherwise acted normal despite the strangeness from the night before. Instead of her cheer uniform, she wore jeans and a sweater.

"Take a picture, it'll last longer," Sabrina said as she opened the locker.

Jamie paused, one hand on her own dial. "Huh?"

Sabrina turned to face her. "You're staring at me. It's really kind of creepy. Were you hoping to see me start blogging when I opened my locker? Or maybe catch me looking guilt-ridden?"

"N-no," Jamie said. She might have been staring, wondering what Sabrina thought of the situation, but words seemed difficult to find. "I, um, I wasn't staring. Just, I dunno, looking in your direction."

"Rrright." Sabrina pulled out a couple textbooks from her locker. "I told you dyke was contagious, but did you listen to me? Noooo…"

Another member of the cheer squad came up behind Sabrina. "Oh my god! 'Brina, I heard on the radio about the superhero fighting bad guys in your front yard! Are you okay?"

Sabrina rolled her eyes. "It was more lame than anything else, Vanessa. Some bimbo dressed like a ninja beating up some of the missing losers."

Jamie winced at the word "bimbo."

The two cheerleaders began walking down the hall past Jamie. "You have to tell me all about it," Vanessa insisted.

Sabrina turned to look at Jamie as she passed her. "Talk at you later, lesbo-bait." Then she turned back to Vanessa. "So, yeah. Last night, I had just gone to bed, when there was like some crazy screaming outside…"

"Jamie?" a boy said, drawing her attention away from Sabrina. Jamie turned to see Justin Hayashi standing next to her. "I don't know if you remember me. I'm—"

"Justin," she interrupted him. "Dharma School, right?"

He looked relieved. "Yes, exactly. It's been a while since you've come to class so I wasn't sure if you—"

"Was there something you wanted?" Jamie asked, her mood turning sour. Thinking about Dharma School didn't brighten her day.

"Well, I was wondering if I could ask for your help. I'm hoping to find out who is behind 2thefairest, and I thought you might be willing to partner up."

"Partner up?" Jamie frowned, turning the dial to open her locker finally. "Why would you care?"

Justin said, "I'm the student body vice president. I feel it's my obligation to look out for the interests of my constituents. And I heard you were looking into it pretty heavily."

Jamie picked out a couple books so that she wouldn't have to come back soon. She'd never thought of the student government actually doing anything, so it seemed weird that Justin would claim that. But she didn't have anything to back it up. For all she knew, he might be right. "Have you been talking to Sabrina?"

"What? Um, no, but I heard about you and your friends following her. That's a pretty heavy level of dedication, and I think you'd be an invaluable ally in this."

"So… what do you want to do? Form a neighborhood watch or something?"

"No, just share information and leads we might find. I don't like where things are going, with the missing students and the gossip blog. It's all so fishy. I know you're not the most social person at the school, but I know a lot of people and can cover that end while you cover it in… whatever method you use."

Jamie closed her locker and shrugged. "Sure. Sounds great."

"Great, I'll talk to you later."

Justin walked away just as Parker walked up holding a slip of paper.

"Did you call number 825?" Parker held up the slip of paper showing those numbers on it.

Jamie looked at her, confused, "What?"

"You had like a line going to talk to you between Sabrina and the veep. And I just happened to still have my number from going to get my driver's license replaced. "

Jamie smiled and shook her head. "Okay..."

"I was really hoping for more of a laugh. 'Cause that was really funny in my head."

Jamie shrugged. "Sorry. Maybe next time. How are you after our failed stakeout?"

"Unabashed. Though I heard Sabrina had a superhuman throwdown in her front yard. I'm kinda bummed we missed that. But on the topic of changing the subject, I was wondering about tonight."

"I'm still planning on going. I didn't change my mind or anything."

"I was just wondering about the Ashley factor."

"What about her? You think she'll cause a problem?"

Parker bit her lower lip and didn't answer.

"Just spit it out," Jamie said.

Parker mumbled, "Are you uncomfortable around me?"

"What? No... Oh, wait. You think I brought Ashley because I'm worried about you...?" Jamie gestured futilely, unable to find the words. "No. I'm really worried about someone coming after her. Seriously, have you seen the pictures of the missing students? She's like the poster child for abduction or whatever is happening to them."

Parker looked relieved. She started to raise her hands up and then swung her arms awkwardly at her side. "Great. I'm glad things aren't... weird between us."

"Hi guys!" Ashley called out from down the hall, waving frantically. Today, she was wearing a blue Glass-Eyed Dolls T-shirt with blue and white bows in her hair.

"Is it just me," Parker said, "or is Ashley getting weirder every day?"

As Ashley came closer she said, "I'm so excited about tonight. I spent, like, an hour deciding what to wear."

"Jeans and a T-shirt?" Parker asked. "That's a bold statement."

"Well, more how to represent the Dolls' colors." Ashley turned to Jamie and asked, "Could I talk to you privately for just a sec?"

Jamie nodded and the two of them stepped away from Parker.

"I don't know if you noticed, but Parker's really fishing for a hug."

"She is?" Jamie asked. Her head suddenly felt light and her she felt her body tense up.

Ashley nodded. "You seem a bit clueless, so I figured I'd let you know just in case."

Ashley walked off towards her locker, leaving Jamie to stare blankly off into nothing. Parker came up and shook Jamie's arm.

"Are you okay?" Parker asked.

"Yeah, I think so." The part of Jamie that hated hugs resisted, but something compelled Jamie to ask, "Did you want a hug?"

A smile instantly appeared on Parker's face. "Well, yeah. But not in, like, a skeezy way. Well, okay. It's a little skeezy. At least not purely motivated. Or platonic. Or whatever. So I'll understand if you aren't interested in a hug from—"

Jamie wrapped her arms around Parker, who hugged her back. Tension slipped away from Jamie. She didn't like hugs, but this felt right. Like two puzzle pieces clicking together. She rested her hands against Parker's back and savored the moment.

"I told you it was contagious," Sabrina said as she walked by, breaking up the moment. Jamie pulled away from Parker, her cheeks feeling warm again. "Hugs are the gateway drug. But if you guys start swapping lesbo spit next to my locker I'm going to talk to the principal."

Parker gestured vaguely away. "I need to... class..."

Jamie nodded, lost for words.

~

Jamie nearly gagged at the dank and musty smell of Bifrost Roller Rink, and it only got worse as she got deeper in. Stale cigarette smoke and the smell of unwashed bodies blended to make the odor of the place overwhelming. With the smell came the noise: the heavy beats of dance music mixed with screaming girls and the clatter of skate wheels on wood.

She rounded the corner to see a mob of girls skating around. Younger girls, some as young as seven, wearing tutus with their helmets, jerseys, and tights, were making their way off of the rink while older girls closer to Jamie's age were warming up. Cleopatra Thunder, who Jamie barely recognized without all of her makeup, spoke to a much older overweight black man in front of the currently closed concession stand. When Cleopatra turned, she saw that the back of her sweatshirt read, "Coach Cleo."

The place also overwhelmed Jamie on the spiritual level. First, there was the obvious: the team spirit for the Glass-Eyed Dolls, a teenage girl who looked very much like a porcelain doll in derby gear, and the spirit of the rink, which looked like an African-American Viking with a giant hammer. Beyond that, the storm smell that Jamie encountered at the West Key Community College filled the air on a spiritual level, cutting through the stink of Bifrost. And then the more subtle. Though they were not manifesting, she could feel that the spirits of the Goblin Town Roller Girls teams were here but dormant. It was as though the lack of their teams meant that they had no place to be.

Someone tackled Jamie with a hug. She only barely identified it as Parker before her defenses kicked in. Jamie returned the hug awkwardly, trying to ignore the pungent smell of Parker's sweat. She didn't think one girl could smell so much like a locker room. With her skates on, Parker towered over Jamie. The skater smiled, pulled out her mouth guard and hooked it in a hole in her helmet.

"I'm so glad you made it!" Parker wore surprisingly little makeup. Even the makeup from earlier had been washed off.

"How could I turn down the chance to see derby behind the scenes?" Jamie said. As Jamie took in the rest of Parker's outfit she added, "Are you wearing short shorts over bicycle shorts over tights?"

Parker looked down and said, "Not exactly. The longer shorts are padded. Required gear for junior skaters." She turned on her skates to show off the back of her shorts. "Besides, how can I say no to shorts that have skeleton hands grabbing my butt? And you didn't say anything about my socks!"

Parker held up one leg that had a knee-high sock that had "NERD" written down the length of it in large letters. Then she raised the other one to show off the sock that said, "GAY."

"And, seriously, how can you judge me for having shorts on the outside? We live in a city filled with superheroes."

"Real superheroes don't wear their underwear on the outside. Seriously, name one who does."

"Magnificent."

"Not real."

"Totally real. His comic book was based after a real superhero in the 1930s."

"That myth was debunked in an interview with Doctor Shadow when he joined the Protectorate. And his whole underwear thing was modeled after a bodybuilder costume, which was only painted to look like it had shorts so it hid his junk."

"What about Superlative?"

"Who?"

"From *Silk Capes.*"

"The soap opera? You actually watch that?"

"I was part of the letter writing campaign to keep it on the air. And Superlative has stopped crimes in real life."

"Do I know you?" Jamie asked. "You just started talking to me and I'm not sure I know you or want to."

Parker stuck her tongue out. "I'm adorable."

Jamie had no idea what to say next, but was saved by the arrival of another skater: Crass Hopper. Parker looked over at her ex-girlfriend nervously, while Jamie tensed for violence.

Crass raised her hand in hesitant greeting. "I don't mean to bother you guys, but I wanted to come over and apologize for how I acted on Friday. I'm not usually that angry. It was just a weird night. Between my random rage and finding someone had left a funky apple in my bag, I felt like I'd been replaced by my evil twin."

"An apple?" Jamie asked. She was getting real sick of apples.

The other girl shrugged. "Yeah. They carved weird symbols on it or something and it leaked juice inside my bag. Mostly it scared the crap out of me. I spent days thinking I'd been tagged by a serial killer or super-villain."

Jamie frowned. She wondered how many other people she'd had a run-in with had been hit with this apple whammy. And how many had had their lives ruined because of some attack on her.

"Oh god," Ashley groaned from the entrance. Jamie, Parker, and Crass all turned to look at her. The newcomer had bent over and covered her face. "I think I'm going to be sick. What is that smell?"

Parker smiled. "It's my new perfume! I call it Pad Funk." To illustrate, Parker lifted up the edge of her elbow pad, took a deep sniff and coughed before forcing a smile.

Ashley gagged, then ran towards the women's bathroom.

Parker shrugged. "Some people are just too delicate for roller derby. C'mon. You can watch me be a badass on skates."

Jamie sat on a folding chair near the edge of the rink while Parker went and did her warm up exercises. Ashley, still looking green around the edges, came out and joined her to watch the practice. The girls varied in skill level. Some fell every ten feet while others, like Parker, skated like they were born to it.

Parker seemed to be pushing herself harder than the others did, waving to Jamie before showing off with some stunt. After a few minutes of that, the other girls began to razz Parker and she focused more on the practice.

Cleopatra began leading the girls through drills, while the older man drifted in and out of the room. Though she never caught them in the act, Jamie could swear that Cleo and the other guy were watching her.

Towards the end of practice, the skaters scrimmaged. Half of the girls donned yellow mesh practice vests and they played against one another. Ashley and Jamie were recruited to time the penalty box, which afforded Jamie the opportunity to talk to Parker for a minute.

"Who's the old guy that keeps skulking around?" Jamie asked.

Parker looked around and, on spotting the man in question, said, "That's Cleo's dad." Her voice sounded funny while she wore her mouth guard.

Jamie looked over at him. He seemed occupied with repairing a pair of skates. "Is there some reason he might be staring at me?"

Parker frowned and shrugged. "Dunno. He's kind of a grumpy old man, so maybe he hates that you're alive? But I think Cleo's mom is dead or something. So it could be he needs a little companionship."

Jamie stuck out her tongue in disgust. "Ugh. That's just gross."

"What can I say?" Parker said, smiling. "I think you're gorgeous and assume everybody wants a piece of you. How much time do I have left?"

"Crap!" Jamie looked back down at the watch and saw that it

was well past the time Parker needed to serve. "Um, Yellow 4321 done!"

With a wink, Parker pushed off the bench used for the penalty box and rejoined the pack.

~

Jamie stared out Glenda's passenger side window, which was streaked with thick raindrops. Through the misty haze of the rain, Jamie could see the clash of light above. Either the lightning had turned weird, or some super-powered battle raged in the skies above Cobalt City.

As she drove, Parker held Jamie's hand. She had slipped her hand into Jamie's as they walked out of Bifrost and they had only let go long enough to get into the car.

"I don't need to have read it," Parker insisted. "If the title *Watching You Sleep* wasn't enough, Haldon actually watches Cassie sleeping before they even start talking to one another. If that doesn't say stalker, I don't know what does."

"But he's so *devoted*," Ashley insisted. "He starts off a little weird, but he's so utterly loyal."

"Help me out here, Jamie," Parker said. "How creepy is *Watching You Sleep*?"

"Is that a movie?" Jamie asked.

"They've made a movie, but it started off as a series of books."

Jamie shrugged. "I don't know much about it. I'm not much of a reader and I don't watch a whole lot of movies."

Parker slammed on the brakes, and Glenda slid a few feet along the rain-slicked street before coming to a stop. She turned to Jamie and shook her by the shoulder. "You are wasting your youth! These are the best years of our lives! Why are you not spending them inside watching TV?!"

A car honked at them from behind before passing around them.

"I don't know." Jamie laughed, startled by Parker's melodramatic reaction. "I guess I just have too much to do."

"I need to fix this," Parker declared as she resumed driving. "Can you find some room in your schedule to spend time doing stuff with me on a regular basis?"

The question hung there between them. Jamie's heart pounded. She knew that there was more implied in that question. Her Kensei identity seemed very far away, while Parker was very close and very warm. She glanced nervously over at Parker, who seemed tense.

"Yes. I think I can," Jamie said.

Parker smiled and squeezed Jamie's hand.

"Ashley, if Parker ever gets too full of herself, you are welcome to dig on her love for *Silk Capes*."

"Not fair. *Silk Capes* is genius, as opposed to derivative vampire porn." Parker pulled the car over. "Casa del Jones! See, Jamie, you won't have Ashley to defend you as I regale you with the glories of *Silk Capes*."

Jamie got out so that she could pull the seat forward and allow Ashley to step out. The rain pelted down, slipping under the collar of her coat and leaving icy chills down her back. Ashley pulled herself out and hurried up the walkway to her door without saying anything.

"Good night, Ashley!" Jamie called. "See you tomorrow?"

Ashley waved without looking back. Jamie got back into the car and shivered. She wondered if that moment with Parker had upset Ashley on some level, and felt a little guilty about the whole thing.

On the way to Jamie's house, Parker grilled Jamie about movies and TV shows she'd seen. Jamie didn't know what sort of criteria Parker used for "must see," but the questions ranged from anime series, sci fi from the BBC and live concerts of assorted performers from the 70s.

When Parker pulled up to the Hattori house she asked, "Want me to walk you to the door?"

Jamie felt like this was another loaded question but said, "Sure."

The two of them scampered across Jamie's front yard, splashing through the puddles in the lawn. Jamie and Parker were laughing by the time they got to Jamie's front porch, soaked from the rain. They stood under the awning in front of the door and shivered.

"I'm glad you came out for the derby stuff," Parker said.

"Me too," Jamie said. "I'm... I'm looking forward to seeing more of you."

Parker smiled in spite of the cold and wet. "Yeah?"

"Yeah." Jamie waited for Parker to say something more, but Parker just smiled. "So..."

"So..."

"Am I missing something? Is this some non-verbal cue that I'm not getting?" Then something clicked in Jamie's head. "Oh."

"I… I should get going," Parker said and turned back to her car.

"Wait."

Parker looked back.

"If you're wanting a kiss goodnight then you're going to have to walk me through it. I've never done this before." Jamie tensed, afraid that she'd misread this and that Parker might just leave.

Instead, Parker stepped closer and looked Jamie in the eye. "Just follow my lead."

Parker parted her lips and leaned forward, kissing Jamie on the lips. Tentative at first, but then with more confidence. Jamie felt like a current ran through her. She leaned into the kiss and grabbed Parker by the waist and drew her closer. A part of her mind boggled that she would run around in a costume for several years when she could have been doing this more. The world seemed to stop and she could have done this forever.

Until the front door opened and she heard her father say, "Oh, sorry."

Jamie broke out of the kiss and looked to see Charles standing in the doorway, a shocked look on his face as he closed the door. When they were alone again, she and Parker both began laughing hysterically. Jamie felt guilty and didn't know how she'd explain this later.

"I think this is a sign I really should go," Parker said with a sly smile. She leaned in and kissed Jamie again on the lips, this time only a brief peck, before running back out towards Glenda.

CHAPTER 10 - KIDS THESE DAYS

Jamie slowly walked down the steps from her bedroom, barely awake. She'd been up all night patrolling after Parker dropped her off, with still no clue what was happening with Karl. On the bright side, she didn't get ambushed again. Hearing her mother's voice from the kitchen woke her up.

"Charles, I'm dead serious," Gloria said. "We need to install better security."

"We have the best we can afford, dear," Charles said. "Besides, I don't think that having better security will give us any better protection. If this killer came here, no one would get here in time. At least not on our budget."

"They have super-powered response."

"First, that's a lot of money. Second, are you changing your tune about super-heroes?"

Jamie walked into the kitchen to see her parents seated at the table, half-finished bowls of cereal and cups of coffee in front of them. The picked-through newspaper lay in the center of the table.

"The people who work for security companies are licensed and bonded security guards, not vigilantes who take the law into their own hands. If they screw up, there are consequences and no mask to hide behind."

Jamie slunk through the kitchen to grab herself a bowl of cereal. She didn't want to get involved with this argument.

"Good morning, sweetie," Gloria said. "Did you have a good time with Parker last night?"

Charles choked on his coffee mid-sip.

Jamie looked over, not sure how much to read into it.

Her dad avoided her gaze, and her mom only looked confused.

"Yeah, I did," Jamie said as she turned back to getting her cereal ready. "Parker's trying to talk me into roller skating."

"That could be fun," her mom said. "It could be a great outlet for your energy."

Jamie shrugged and went to sit down at the kitchen table.

Gloria studied her daughter for a moment before changing the topic. "Do you know Courtney Canvil?"

"Not directly," Jamie said between bites of food. She didn't think it a good time to mention brawling with her in front of Sabrina's house. "I saw her name among the missing students. I've seen her picture. Why? Did they learn something?"

"No, but a super-powered person murdered her parents." Gloria tapped one of the newspapers.

"A *possible* super-powered person," Charles emphasized. "They're still examining clues."

"Fine." Gloria glared at her husband. "Then it was a small person who may or may not have superpowers that punched hard enough to break bone and beat Mr. and Mrs. Canvil to death."

"Someone properly trained can do that. I think you're blowing this out of proportion."

"I think the facts in the paper speak for themselves."

"I think there are a lot of unknowns. And it's not as though this house is undefended."

Gloria frowned. "I'm not interested in considering this option."

"Home defense is not the same as vigilantism. Jamie's proven she can defend herself and—"

"No!" Gloria slammed her hand down on the table. "We have an agreement, Charles Hattori. Think carefully about what you say next."

Charles crumpled, whatever he was going to say lost. He stood with his empty bowl and cup and took them to the sink.

"Do I get to know what this agreement is?"

Her parents responded in unison, "No."

Jamie slouched and poked at the remains of her cereal. This was not a good start to the day.

~

The stares and whispers followed Jamie through the halls as she headed towards her locker. A few times she heard the words "dyke" and "girl on girl," and a knot of dread and confusion built in her stomach. This was not helped by seeing Parker standing by Jamie's locker looking guilty.

"I suppose you're really mad at me," Parker said.

Jamie glanced towards other students who lingered nearby. "I don't know what's going on. Should I be mad at you?"

"2thefairest posted a picture of us last night."

"Of us? Okay."

"From your front porch."

"My front porch? Oh! Oh." Jamie looked at her locker rather than look at Parker or the gaping audience that surrounded them.

Someone took hold of Jamie's arm and began to pull at her. Jamie looked over, anticipating an attack. Instead she saw Sabrina, her jaw clenched and eyes hard.

"We need to talk," the cheerleader said. Parker tried to interrupt Sabrina, but Sabrina just raised a hand to halt her. "Whatever you're going to say, shut the hell up, Parker. C'mon, Jamie, let's find somewhere private to talk."

Jamie let herself be led to the girls' restroom. Sabrina stopped her at the sink and banged on the two stall doors. "Private meeting. Wipe and leave."

Girls hurried out of the two stalls, each pausing to glance with pity at Jamie. Apparently this was not the first time Sabrina had pulled this stunt.

When the door had closed behind the departing students, Sabrina wheeled to face Jamie. "You need to stay the hell away from Parker if you have any sense of self-preservation."

"Wait, what? Why the hell should you care?" Jamie wasn't certain she wanted a lasting anything with Parker, but she knew it was none of Sabrina's business.

"I've seen Parker destroy lives. She has an agenda and she doesn't care if people get hurt. She's spoiled and irresponsible and possibly insane. I tried to hit you with shame, but apparently you're too dumb to get the hint. If you want a likely suspect for your stupid blog, I'd name Parker. She's just petty enough to do it."

"You're calling someone else petty?"

Sabrina frowned in confusion. "Are you trying to say I'm

petty?"

"What? Are you too dumb to get it?"

Sabrina pursed her lips, took a deep breath and walked towards the exit. "Remember, I warned you about this." Outside she called out to people standing nearby, "Don't you have someplace else you're supposed to be?"

Jamie left the bathroom cautiously. Surprisingly few people lingered nearby, and everyone made a point of not looking at the bathroom door or Jamie. She looked around for Parker, but couldn't see her anywhere nearby.

~

Kensei watched the Canvil home from the tree across the street, waiting to make sure nothing bad lurked in the house. It was a single story brick building with a one car garage and a finely manicured lawn. The door had been broken in and yellow police tape crisscrossed over the dark hole left behind. She saw no sign of a yard spirit, but some sort of spirit seemed to be moving around inside the house.

When no cars remained in sight, Kensei crept across the street. She avoided the pools of light provided by street lamps and made her way to the front door. She detached just enough of the police tape to allow her to squeeze through the rest and enter the house. From deeper within, she heard a man quietly sobbing. She took each step with great caution, barely able to see in the darkness of the house. But she had no trouble seeing the spirit as he stood in one of the bedrooms.

"José?" Kensei called out, because he looked much like the spirit at the Alvarez house, though more Mediterranean than Hispanic. Some spirits, like Ungyo and Agyo, had the same name when they fulfilled the same role in multiple locations. If she went to a different church of her tradition, there would be another Ungyo and Agyo, but with different personalities.

But this spirit seemed much thinner than José, emaciated even, with gray hair and an ashen hint to his skin. His robes hung in tatters around him. But still, she sensed that he was very similar to the other spirit.

The spirit looked up, his cheeks wet with tears. He shook his head. "No, my name is Giuseppe, but I understand the confusion."

"What happened here, Giuseppe?"

"The devil took his due," the spirit said.

Kensei frowned behind her mask. She hoped he meant metaphorically and not the literal devil. She didn't need more supernatural threats. "Can you give me more details?"

"Mark, the man of the house, was not a gentle man. He often hurt Courtney."

"Abused her?" Kensei asked.

The spirit nodded. "It is awful to be the protector of a home and not able to protect," the spirit said. "I have pushed back all manner of dark spirits that threatened to cause harm here, but I could do nothing for the physical threats. I am fortunate some choices have been taken out of my hands."

"What do you mean?"

"Despite his rough nature, Mark and his wife, Jessica, were heartbroken by the loss of sweet Courtney. Mark could not understand how there could be such monsters who would harm his little girl. Jessica feared that Mark had gone too far and had to hide Courtney's body. She worried about both the fate of her daughter and the possibility that she shared a bed with a murderer."

"Courtney's mom knew what Mark did?"

Guissepe nodded. Kensei could only look away, feeling like she'd fallen down a dark hole by coming here. This whole thing got worse the longer it went on. She hated this part of her power. Every spirit bore the scars of every awful thing that happened under its domain, and could tell her about them. Alley spirits were not as bashful as house spirits. It was why Kensei didn't hang up her mask and just give up: because for every hurt in the world, a spirit bore the bruises and bled from the cuts. She just couldn't ignore that.

Guissepe continued. "Courtney returned changed. I had heard rumors of such things from the Old Country, but had not actually encountered one before."

"A *strix*?"

Guissepe nodded. "The family heirlooms in this house remember hearing old stories about such things, dark creatures lurking beneath Rome. Under normal circumstances, I could have resisted her entering. If she managed to push past me, I could attack the *strix* that possessed her directly. I do not know that it would have been right, but it would have been within my power to do so."

"Doesn't she live here?"

"Yes, but the *strix* is the servant of a pagan god. This house is consecrated to our Lord in Heaven, and such devil spawn is not welcome here."

"How did she get in then?"

"When Mark saw her alive and well, he grew upset. He was angry and accused her of causing them to worry for no reason. So he said, 'Get in here right now.'"

Kensei closed her eyes. "He invited her in."

"As the man of the house, it is his right. And retribution for his sins caught up with him. If you see Courtney, could you tell her I'm sorry?"

"Definitely," Kensei said.

The spirit nodded and faded from view. Kensei made her way back out to the front door. As she scanned to see if she was clear to leave, she saw an owl perched atop a telephone pole. She sensed that the bird was looking at her.

"Courtney?" she called out, trying not to sound too loud.

The owl bobbed its head.

"I spoke to the spirit of the house," Kensei said. "He's sorry he could not do more to help you."

The owl tilted its head.

"And I'm sorry I didn't know about this. I understand why you did this, but I hope this is the end. Please… just help me stop Eris and come back to the world."

The owl launched from the telephone pole, silent wings beating as it flew off into the night. Kensei began the long walk home.

CHAPTER 11 - NEW THINGS COME TO LIGHT

The next day, Jamie saw little of her friends throughout the morning. She wondered if people had begun avoiding her, and how much of that was because of Sabrina. At lunch, while Jamie tried to figure out what the breaded meat item was beneath the gravy, Ashley set her tray down next to Jamie and said, "May I sit here?"

"No one else has claimed it so far."

"You doing okay?" Ashley asked. "I saw the photo of you and Parker."

"It is what it is." Jamie didn't mention how much she'd been mentally chanting the *nembutsu* to try and stay calm.

"I have another lead for the blog," Ashley said.

Jamie knew she should be excited, but after the previous day she just couldn't find the energy. Especially after Sabrina's random warning. "Is it Parker?"

"What? No. At least, I don't think it is. Do you think it's Parker?"

"It could be anyone. I don't know. Who's your lead?"

"Travis Lambros."

Jamie shook her head. "I don't know who that is, but I have reason to believe that 2thefairest is a girl."

Ashley frowned. "You do? How did you figure that much out?"

"I have my ways."

"It could still be that Travis is a lead. Last night 2thefairest posted something that I thought only Travis and I knew about, but maybe he told other people."

"I don't check the blog very often. It, um, just puts me in a bad mood. What did 2thefairest post?"

Ashley scooted closer to Jamie and whispered, "Travis and I met online and dated for a while. When he finally met me face to face, I… I didn't live up to his expectations. It ended badly. The whole experience is recounted on the blog."

"Okay, but he goes to a different school, right?" Jamie asked.

"Yes."

"Then how does he know so much about people at this school?"

Ashley shrugged. "If you're right and the blogger is a girl, she could have gotten the story from him somehow."

"You don't think she just got it through the grapevine?"

Ashley shook her head. "The details are too good. I'm sure the person who did it had access to an original account of the story."

Jamie wondered how subtle 2thefairest could be with her apple whammy. She'd seen rage, but could the blogger manage a really fine manipulation?

"Sure," Jamie said. "I'll look into it later tonight."

"Okay. If you need any help, let me know."

Though she planned on doing this under the guise of Kensei, Jamie said, "Sure thing."

Justin came up with his tray and asked to join them as well. Once he was settled in he asked, "How goes the research into 2thefairest?"

"We totally have a new lead," Ashley said.

Justin smiled. It made Jamie think he was a politician in training. "Great to hear. I knew I was right to come to you about this."

"Ashley's just a regular Nancy Drew," Jamie said. "I'm her goofy sidekick of color." The other two didn't laugh at the joke. Jamie wondered if she took things too far.

"Do you need help with it?" Justin asked.

Jamie snorted out a laugh. "Are you offering to protect me?"

Justin laughed. "No, I think you've proven you don't need protection. But I find I'm really good with people and could maybe grease the wheels of communication."

"Wasn't 'Grease the Wheels of Communication' your campaign slogan?" Jamie asked.

"No, it was actually 'Grease the Wheels of Bureaucracy.' That and 'Justin Time.'"

"Greasing many wheels of bureaucracy?"

"No, turns out the job is mostly just organizing fundraisers and events. Speaking of, we have a fifty-fifty raffle going on right now to help pay for Homecoming."

"I think I'll pass. I've made it my whole life without going to a single dance. I'd like to continue this winning trend. I'll save my dollar."

"Wait, did you just veer us off the topic of your lead?" Justin laughed again. "That was pretty smooth. But seriously, I'd really like to help."

"Travis is up in Morriston," Ashley said. "If you have a car, that would be really helpful."

Jamie groaned. "Wow, the heart of suburbia."

"I'd think you'd have a car by now, Jamie," Justin said.

"My parents aren't that rich. And I don't have my license."

Justin looked stricken. "How can you be a senior and not have your license?"

"Getting a license takes practice. Practice requires time. Time is something I rarely have much of."

"Well, I'll see if I can borrow my mom's minivan for the afternoon."

Parker chimed in from behind them, "Or I could just drive y'all." She set her tray down. Today's look involved a Last Laff Roller Derby T-shirt that had been split in half along the seam and then reattached with small safety pins.

Despite all the frustrations of the day before, Jamie still smiled at the sight of Parker. Something felt right seeing her again. "We're getting the band back together?"

"It's been almost a week since I've stalked someone in Glenda. Why not?"

"Great!" Justin said. "We're getting the band back together!"

"Yeah, except you're John Goodman," Parker said. When the rest of the table gave her blank looks, Parker added, "*Blues Brothers*, people. And the unfortunate sequel. Get some culture."

~

Morriston had few redeeming qualities, unless you enjoyed

going to the mall. It wasn't like the Hollows, where you could get murdered just for breathing. Instead, it was an empty sprawl of subdivisions and strip malls. There was little to encourage non-residents to go there.

But there Jamie sat, riding shotgun in Glenda and heading northeast into the area. Parker had picked up Justin and Ashley first. They were both in the back when they arrived at Jamie's house, depriving Jamie of the opportunity to try and talk to Parker.

Travis's house lay nested at the end of a cul-de-sac, a two-story white house in a trim and proper neighborhood. Only a faint sprinkling of leaves lay on the ground, as opposed to the thick, mushy carpet on the Hattori lawn.

Parker stretched as she got out of the car, her shirt riding up and baring the edge of her ribs. Jamie noticed and stumbled as she got out of the car. She hoped that no one had seen.

"Think we look like a gang?" Parker asked.

"Only a really lame one," Jamie said as she helped Ashley climb out of the back seat.

Justin looked around. "Why would they think we're a gang?"

Jamie and Parker both shook their heads and headed up the winding walkway to the front door. Justin and Ashley hurried to catch up.

"Care to do the honors, Mr. Veep?" Parker asked.

Justin stepped forward and rang the doorbell. Jamie glanced over at him and had to admit that he did dress for success. His button-up shirt and khakis probably looked more respectable than Parker and Jamie in their T-shirts and tattered jeans.

An older woman opened the door and looked at them. She looked tired and fragile. This didn't feel right to Jamie. She glanced around to try and spot the spirit of the house and didn't see anything. It wasn't conclusive, but it did nag at her.

Justin cleared his throat. "Hello, are you Mrs. Lambros?"

"You're not Mormons are you, or looking for money?"

"What? No. We're just wondering if Travis is home."

That pushed her last nerve. Her face crumpled and she leaned against the doorjamb, sobbing.

"I'm sorry, is this a bad time?" Justin looked around for some sort of advice.

"He's… he's been missing for a few weeks now. I heard that other kids in the city have disappeared recently, but I couldn't understand why he had to go too. Were we not good enough parents?"

As if in response, someone screamed in rage from the street, prompting the four teens to turn and look in that direction. In the middle of the cul-de-sac, someone wearing a hooded sweatshirt stood clutching his head.

"Travis?" Mrs. Lambros called out.

Travis responded to his name by charging at the house. Sensing something was wrong, Jamie said in a quiet voice, "Everyone get inside and don't invite him in."

Justin looked at her funny, "What, you think he's some sort of vamp—"

Travis cut off Justin by picking him up and throwing him back towards the lawn. The student body vice president landed with a hard thud. Jamie used that distraction to punch Travis in the solar plexus, follow up with a roundhouse to the face, and then a kick to the groin.

"What are you doing?" Mrs. Lambros screamed as Ashley and Parker pushed her deeper into the house. "What are you doing to my son?!"

Jamie dodged a clumsy punch from Travis, using his momentum to aid her kick to his ribs, followed by an elbow to the base of his skull. All of her blows barely seemed to faze him. While doubled over, he picked her up by the waist and lifted her sideways off the ground.

Jamie scrambled to find anything sensitive she could hit to slow him down before he did something awful, but could not connect with anything. Parker ran out of the house, dropped low and hip-checked him to throw him off balance. He let go of Jamie as he tried to regain his balance but ending up falling anyway.

Travis half pulled himself up as he began to change into an owl. Jamie sprang to her feet and tackled him, finding that she now held a flapping and biting bird that threatened to lift them both off the ground. Parker dogpiled on top of Jamie and they both pinned down the owl until Jamie could punch it unconscious. When it finally went limp, it turned back into the prone form of Travis.

Jamie noticed that the pocket on his hoodie held a large, round bulge. With a bitten, bleeding arm, she reached in and pulled out an apple with the Greek writing carved into it.

"What is it?" Parker asked. "Wait, that looks like the apple from

2thefairest.com."

"Doesn't it, though?" Jamie said.

~

The police arrived within minutes and began taking statements. Jamie half expected to be carted out of the neighborhood and have to call her parents from the police station, but Mrs. Lambros gave a reasonable account of events and didn't offer to press charges.

An ambulance came to transport Justin to the hospital. He'd broken his arm and a few ribs. His parents were meeting him there. Travis was taken in for questioning, with a strange old man riding up front in the squad car. A paramedic bandaged up Jamie's bite marks and told her to have her parents take her to see their doctor. Then Jamie, Ashley, and Parker waited for their parents to pick them up.

"So," Jamie said, sitting with Parker on the hood of Glenda. Parker slipped her hand into Jamie's, while Ashley chatted with the police officers by the curb.

"So," Parker replied.

"I talked to Sabrina yesterday."

Parker nodded. "I noticed. What did she have to say?"

"Warned me to stay away from you. Said she'd watched you destroy friend's lives."

"Ah. I see."

"So why did you disappear while I was in there?"

"I didn't know what she was going to say. We share a secret, and she holds the key. I didn't know what she'd tell you or if you'd want to talk to me again."

"Are you 2thefairest?"

Parker frowned. "Do you really think I'm like that?"

"I don't really know much about you at all, but you did say early on that vengeance runs in your family."

Parker winced and laughed. "Yeah, I guess I did say that."

"And?"

"It's something my birth mom says, especially when I'm pissed off. 'Well, vengeance runs in your family.' Since she never claims it for herself, I'm guessing that it refers to the long-lost Mr. Fiorenza who helped spawn me."

"What about the blog?"

"I'm going to say 'no.' I'm not behind the blog. I'll let you decide if you believe me or not."

"I'm going to need more than that to rule you out entirely," Jamie said. She meant it as joking, and hoped it sounded that way.

Parker slipped her hand into Jamie's. "Well, I have in mind a fabulous plan for tomorrow night. I'm thinking an all-night marathon of *Revolutionary Girl Utena* while I ply you with Mountain Dew and Skittles."

Jamie laughed, wondering if the cops noticed her holding hands with a girl. She still had her doubts about Parker but at the moment she just couldn't take them seriously. "How about just an evening marathon? I can't be hanging out all night with you."

"Sounds like a date. Hey, that looks like your parents. Should I go say 'Hi'?"

Jamie sighed. "Probably not. This is where I'm going to get an ass chewing for getting into another fight."

"Amateur!" Parker said, shoving against Jamie. "This is where you break their rage with a friend that they won't lose their temper in front of. Distract them a bit. Do they know about the blog thing?"

"My mom doesn't, so don't bring it up. She... she wouldn't understand."

Parker sprang off the hood and began walking to where Mr. and Mrs. Hattori were getting out of their car. Jamie followed. The stern-faced parents looked surprised to see Parker.

"Mr. and Mrs. Hattori, I just wanted to take a moment to thank you for Jamie saving my life. When we came here to meet with Ashley's friend, we didn't expect him to have turned into some berserker shapeshifter that would try to kill us. She really saved my life today."

Gloria looked startled by the thanks. "Well, we really like you, Parker. We wouldn't want you to get hurt."

"I'm touched that you think so highly of me," Parker said. "Say, Jamie was going to come over and watch some anime with me tomorrow. Is that okay? I promise to have her home at a reasonable hour."

"Sure, that should be fine."

"Great. Oh, here come my moms. I'll see you tomorrow, Jamie." Before Jamie knew what to do, Parker kissed her on the lips. Jamie kissed back on reflex, realizing belatedly that she hadn't told her mom about this.

Jamie looked at her mom, who only stared slackjawed and wide-eyed at her daughter. Her dad was already walking towards the car. They got in without another word and began driving.

Normally, the lecture from her mom would come at this point, but they rode in silence for several minutes. When her mother did speak, Jamie didn't think to expect the obvious question from her mom. "Jamie, are you and Parker dating?"

Jamie hesitated, realizing she didn't have a good answer. She felt as though if she said yes, she'd be committed to that answer forever. "I don't know."

"Well, let me know if I need to meet with her parents."

No lecture on fighting came that day.

CHAPTER 12 - WORKING FOR THE WEEKEND

Parker's stepmother, who insisted on being called Laura, poked her head in while Parker swapped out DVDs. "How you girls doing?"

"I'm doing fine," Jamie said. She sat on Parker's bed, her back against the wall. The room was small and cluttered, filled mostly with a twin size bed, piles of laundry in various stages of dirty, video games and DVDs. Plus the piles of empty Mountain Dew cans and Skittles wrappers that Jamie and Parker had left lying around.

The walls and shelves were filled with superhero memorabilia, mostly the cheap Protectorate collectibles once sold at the headquarters gift shop: posters, action figures, buttons. Most of the decorations represented the high profile women. Worm Queen, Wild Kat, Libertine, and Velvet dominated the room with their officially licensed merchandise. But a few men made the cut, mostly Huntsman, with a bit of Knockabout and Stardust. Jamie's room had been similarly decorated once, before her mom turned against superheroes. Now all that remained were a few old anime posters and Hello Kitty toys.

Parker jumped back onto the bed, nearly bouncing Jamie off in the progress. "Yeah, I think we're good." After Laura had returned to the living room, Parker asked, "You ready to start another disk?"

"Hold on, I think I need to get rid of some Mountain Dew,"

Jamie said, clawing her way out of the bed. "Or possibly puke."

Parker frowned. "Puke?"

"I'm not used to this much sugar anymore."

"You sugar binge like an old woman. But I'll warn you now. You want to figure out which bodily function before you get going. If you guess wrong, it turns ugly."

Jamie shook her head and wobbled through the door and down the hall. She'd seen this part on her nickel tour when they first arrived at Parker's house. The tour had been hurried, as Parker hadn't wanted to waste precious viewing time with unnecessary things. Jamie took her time, looking at the pictures of Parker arrayed around the hallway between the bedrooms and the bathroom.

School photos from kindergarten through senior year lined the wall, with other photos of Parker and family mixed in between. One that caught her eye was a group photo from summer camp, four years earlier. She picked out Parker quickly, even though her hair was black in the picture. A couple other girls looked half familiar and she had to look in the legend to positively identify them: Sabrina Alvarez and Ashley Jones. None of the three girls stood next to the other in the picture.

Bookshelves lined each side of the hallway, making the path seem tight and cluttered. *Watching You Sleep* and its sequels caught Jamie's eye, as well as yearbooks from middle and high school. New age books from *Drawing Down the Moon* to *Qabbalistic Tarot* filled other portions, as well as books for *Dungeons & Dragons* and *Vampire: The Masquerade*.

Jamie spotted one book titled *Oriental Adventures* and pulled it out to look at it, knocking off a couple books that had been wedged in on top. *Oriental Adventures* was apparently for "Advanced" *Dungeons & Dragons*. The cover featured a samurai riding on a guardian lion squaring off against a ninja in front of a Chinese pagoda. Something about the guardian lion caused her a twinge of anxiety, but otherwise the whole thing was so bad that she rolled her eyes and put it back on the shelf.

While picking up the fallen books, the last book caught her eye. It was black with an apple embossed on the front with gold foil. The apple had a slice cut out of it and the letter K on the side. The title was *Principia Discordia*. She flipped it over to read the back but only read the first sentence before she had to stop: "This book is the bible of Discordianism . . . the worship of Eris, the goddess of Chaos."

She almost peed right there.

Jamie put the book carefully back and wondered if it would look too suspicious if she just ran. At the very least, she still had to go to the bathroom. She made it to the bathroom before realizing that Parker's last name was probably Italian. And Italians had once been Romans. And Romans had poached a whole bunch of gods from the Greeks.

She fought off the urge to run again, despite her sudden willingness to pee her pants, and just went to the bathroom. When she was done, she had calmed down enough that she decided to play it cool.

When Jamie came back to Parker's room, the mattress had been turned sideways and pulled halfway off the bed. The blankets hung over the sides of the mattress like curtains around the hollow space underneath. Parker was nowhere in sight.

"Hello...?"

Parker pushed aside the blankets to look out from under the mattress.

"What are you doing?" Jamie asked.

"I got bored waiting. So I changed clothes a few times."

"I was only gone for a few minutes."

"I did it really fast. And then I got bored again. So I turned my bed into a fort."

Jamie didn't know what to make of this. Any fear she had of Parker being either Eris or an agent of Eris was swept aside in a wave of confusion. Would Parker even be capable of plotting against someone? Jamie had to admit, though, that Parker definitely embodied chaos.

"So are we done watching *Utena*?" Jamie asked.

"No! No. I'm just entertaining myself."

Parker climbed out from underneath the bed and put the mattress back where it belonged. She had previously been wearing a Foster the People T-shirt and jeans, but now she wore a neon green swimsuit with pajama pants covered in penguins and footballs.

Once they were settled in, Parker started the next disc. Parker snuggled in close to Jamie and held her hand. While Parker idly stroked Jamie's fingers with her thumb, Jamie wondered why she'd have to be so happy with her possible arch nemesis.

They watched an episode in silence. As the credits rolled, Parker said, "I love this series. I got my mom to pay for fencing lessons for me because I wanted to be Utena Tenjou so bad."

"I didn't know you fenced," Jamie said.

"Not any more. I got too aggressive in competition and my mom made me stop. Derby has been on a trial basis to see if I've mellowed with age."

"And have you...?"

"Oh, yeah. Totally. I've only gotten into one fight playing derby."

This did not reassure Jamie at all. Then an idea struck her.

"Were you still wanting to go to church with me?"

"Hell yeah!" Parker straightened up, pausing the DVD. "When?"

"My parents usually go to Sunday service. We could go this Sunday and I can show you around a bit."

"That would be awesome! When and where?"

"I'll check to make sure my parents are going and then I'll give you a call."

"Thank you." Parker sprang to the side to tackle Jamie and kiss her on the cheek. "I really appreciate you sharing this with me. Hey, did you have any plans for Homecoming?"

Jamie hesitated. She hadn't been to a dance in her life. "No?"

"Would you be willing to go with me?"

Jamie froze. On the one hand, Jamie knew this could be a trap. On the other hand, she was beginning to think that she might like Parker enough to attend a school function with her. She didn't know how committed she felt to this, but Parker looked very hopeful. "Um, sure. I guess that could be... fun...?"

"Rockin'."

~

Agyo pranced around on the steps as Jamie walked up towards the church doors with her family and other members of the church. The guardian spirit of the church was not the only one to note her presence, as several other people furtively glanced her way.

"Oh, man!" the spirit said. "I didn't think I'd ever see you come to service again. Ungyo will be so happy when he sees you!"

Jamie tried to smile encouragingly, not able to really talk to him with an audience.

The sound of running pulled Jamie's attention toward the street. Parker ran up the stairs two at a time. She'd dressed up for service, with a knee-length charcoal skirt, pale gray tights, patent leather Mary Janes, white blouse, black cardigan, and a men's tie. Her hair had even been tamed down. Jamie couldn't believe this was the same person. Jamie felt shabby in comparison, with her jeans, black T-shirt, and Nikes.

"I was worried I was late," Parker said, breathing hard from her run. "Parking sucked and I ended up down the street a ways."

"You're just in time," Jamie said.

Parker smiled and slipped her hand into Jamie's. The public display of affection surprised Jamie, adding self-consciousness to her other worries for the morning. But she didn't want to make a scene, so she just smiled and led Parker up the steps to catch up with Charles and Gloria. While her father pointedly ignored her and Parker, Gloria looked back and smiled.

"Parker, how good to see you again. I understand you're responsible for Jamie attending service today. You are turning out to be quite the positive influence for her."

"'Positive Influence' is actually my middle name," Parker said. "I'm named after my Great Aunt Positive Influence."

Gloria laughed and continued into the church. Jamie guided Parker through bowing as they entered the church and showed her how to wear the *Monto Shikisho*. Ungyo dithered about her, going through the motions of patting Jamie on the back.

When Jamie's parents went up to make offerings to Amida Buddha, Jamie asked, "Mom? Could you show Parker how to make an offering? I have to hit the ladies room."

"Of course," Gloria said. "Parker, come with us if you're interested."

Parker gave Jamie a confused look but fell into step with Gloria while Jamie ran down the hall to the restroom. Once in a stall, Jamie whispered tersely, "Agyo, where are you?"

From the other side of the stall door Agyo said, "I really don't feel comfortable in here. Don't you need privacy?"

"I'm not peeing. I just came in here so I could talk to you."

"Could you pick a less awkward place next time?"

"Sure. Fine. Did you see the girl I came in with?"

"Parker? Yeah. She's a cutie. Is that your girlfriend?"

"Maybe. But is she Eris?"

"You think she's Eris?"

"Yes. That's why I'm here today!"

"Well, if she's a Greek goddess of discord, she's hiding it really well."

Someone came in to use the other stall in the bathroom, forcing Jamie to wait on any other questions. Jamie checked for Parker's shoes in the other stall, then listened to every intimate detail of the other restroom occupant before the woman finally washed her hands and left.

"Does she worship Eris at least?" Jamie asked.

"As far as I can tell, she's kind of a non-denominational new agey type."

"Are you sure?" Jamie asked.

"Well, there are ways to trick me, but I've seen a lot of the new agey types come in and she sort of matches the profile. She's got a little more greed, hatred, and delusion in her than other people. But it's nothing remarkable."

Jamie rested her head against the stall wall, whimpering.

"You seem disappointed. Did you want your girlfriend to be a bad guy?"

"I just wanted to be done with all of this. Crap. I should get back out there before the service starts."

Jamie made it back just as the church bell rang to begin service. Whispers broke out as Jamie took her seat on the pew between her parents and Parker. The two people that Jamie least wanted to see, Mr. and Mrs. Sohda, looked back at her. They looked older than the last time she had seen them, five years before. They had fewer dark circles under their eyes but their hair had begun to gray. Jamie turned her attention to the service book, trying to pretend they weren't there.

This was a mistake. Not only was there no indicator that Parker was connected with Eris, but now she had to face the Sohdas.

She spent the hour of the service going through the motions, not really paying much attention. She chanted, she sang *gathas*, she forced a laugh in response to Reverend Nishijima's jokes during his dharma talk. But inside, all she could remember were the accusing looks and the questions she couldn't answer.

After the announcements at the end, people began to stand. Some mingled, others headed out the main doors. Ungyo stood at the exit, trying to bless people so that the positive influence of the dharma would stay with them.

"Girls," Gloria said, "did you want to go to the Dharma Exchange in back? There's tea and cookies."

"I maintain a strong pro-cookie platform," Parker said. "I'd love to."

Jamie took off her *Monto Shikisho* and shook her head. "I need to get out of here. Sorry. I'll walk home."

She saw a look of understanding in her mom's face just before she turned and double timed it out the main doors. Agyo appeared on the steps in front of her, waving and calling for her attention. Jamie ignored him and hit the street at a run. She didn't have a plan, she just went. Down side streets, through alleys and across parking lots.

When she grew tired of people staring at her, she turned down an alley and leapt up to the top of a dumpster so she could reach the fire escape ladder. On the roof, she felt comfortable again. She walked over to the edge and looked down at the city.

She didn't know how much time had passed when Parker said, "Holy crap, you're hard to keep up with."

Jamie looked back to see Parker dragging herself up the ladder to the roof, gasping for air. In one hand she held her Mary Janes. She couldn't believe Parker had followed her this far. "What are you doing here?"

Parker bent over, hands resting on her thighs, chest heaving. "Following you."

"I thought you were getting cookies."

"Yeah, but I watched the girl I worship and adore look upset all through the service and then run off unexpectedly at the end. I couldn't just go eat cookies guilt free. I had to see what was wrong."

"Did you run in heels?"

Parker nodded. "I'm going to regret that, probably. I had to take them off to get up here. I just couldn't manage the dumpster with them on. How did you do it?"

Jamie stared at Parker. She felt overwhelmed by the thought that Parker would follow her all this way just to see what was wrong. Tears ran down Jamie's cheeks. It made the lie that much harder.

"I used to do a lot of parkour. I don't usually tell people because they make all sorts of weird assumptions."

Parker walked up and brushed away some of the tears before resting her hands on the back of Jamie's neck. "So what do you need? A hug? An ear? Me to go away?"

Jamie leaned in, wrapped her arms arm Parker's waist and rested her head on the other girl's shoulder. They stood that way for a while before Jamie spoke.

"When I was growing up in the church, my parents put me in Dharma School so I could learn about the Dharma and make some friends. I was the only kid in my age group who was not full Japanese. I was taking gymnastics at the time, so I was always climbing on stuff. One of the girls, her name was Alexis Sohda, said my name should be *Saru* because I liked to climb and jump on things."

Parker whispered, "That's… 'monkey,' right?"

Jamie nodded. "When I told my parents, my mom lost it. It reminded her too much of 'porch monkey.' They met with Reverend Nishijima and Alexis's parents. Alexis got into a whole lot of trouble. And of course it just made her dislike me and take it out on me."

Parker squeezed tighter for a moment but said nothing.

"It went on for years. The rest of the kids in our group still tried to be friends with me, but it was hard when Alexis stirred up so much trouble. So I ended up left out more often than not. When I was twelve I was invited over to Justin's birthday party. The adults all went off and socialized while we hung out in the family room."

Jamie hesitated, trying to find the force of will to keep talking. Parker waited quietly for her. When Jamie finally spoke, her voice cracked a few times before she cleared her throat and started again.

"We were playing truth or dare. Someone dared me and Alexis to go into a closet and make out for a few minutes."

Parker tensed up when Jamie said this, but said nothing.

"I remember the door closing with a click. And then I was in the hospital. I found out that a few minutes after we went into the closet, we both started screaming at the top of our lungs. When our parents pulled us out, we were both catatonic. I woke a week later but Alexis still hasn't woken up."

Parker stroked Jamie's back while holding her tighter.

"The worst part isn't knowing that something weird happened and I don't remember it. It's that everyone blames me for it. Especially Alexis's parents. Every time I went to service or Dharma School, people would just stare. They wouldn't talk to me. They'd just stare."

The two girls stood in silence on the rooftop, holding each other close. Jamie didn't mind that Parker said nothing. She didn't know that anything could be said to make the day better.

Jamie also didn't tell the rest of the story: That she started seeing spirits after that day. From the gaunt and creepy spirit of the mental hospital she'd been in to the wounded and bleeding spirits of the worst alleys in Karlsburg. She didn't mention what it was like for her to see things, certain she was losing her mind, or what it was like to be approached by the spirit of the neighborhood, who begged for her to help stop the pain and suffering in the neighborhood.

For different reasons, she also did not mention that her grandfather died while she lay catatonic.

Without speaking, they let go of one another and made their way down the ladder to the street.

CHAPTER 13 - SUDDEN BUT INEVITABLE BETRAYAL

Monday morning, Jamie and Parker walked through the school's halls together. Parker kept slipping her hand into Jamie's, but Jamie kept pushing Parker away while people glanced furtively at them.

Finally Parker asked, "Is there some new secret you think people will learn if they see us holding hands?"

Jamie shook her head. "I'm just not a fan of PDA. It's nobody's business what I'm doing."

"I totally agree that it's nobody's business, but I came to a very different answer about that."

As they drew near to Jamie's locker, they noticed Justin talking to Sabrina. Justin had his arm in a cast and purpling bruises on his face. Jamie wouldn't have thought much of them talking if Sabrina and Justin hadn't both looked up at her with guilt on their faces before Sabrina turned and left.

Justin came over, a wide forced smile on his face. "Hey guys! What did I miss after I went to the hospital?"

"*Anime,*" Parker said. "Hot girl-on-girl action featuring me and Jamie. Sunday service at Cobalt City Buddhist Church."

The last startled Justin. "You went to service?"

"Yes," Jamie said, in a tone that she hoped invited no further questions.

It seemed to have worked. "How about the 2thefairest? Did

you find out anything else about the blog?"

"Nothing that panned out."

Justin nodded. "Well, keep me posted. And let me know if you need any help."

"Will do." As Justin walked away Jamie said to Parker, "I need to step outside and make a call. See you after school?"

Parker nodded and gave Jamie a peck on the cheek before Jamie could stop her and ran off through the crowds in the hall.

Jamie walked out a nearby door to the school lawn. She pulled her cell phone out and went through the motions of making a call. After a second she said, "Abe, where the hell are you?"

"What do you want, Jamie?" the spirit said from next to her.

Jamie looked over to see the flannel clad ex-president standing while students walked past and through him without seeing him. "What's up with Justin and Sabrina? They seem to be plotting."

"You're talking to me again, are you?"

"Don't be a dork. You bagged on me. Are you in a helpful mood?"

"Will the offerings continue?"

"Sure."

"Justin only offered to help with the investigation because Sabrina asked him to help. She didn't want to offer to help herself."

"What? Why the hell would she do that?"

"If she had offered to help, how would you have reacted?"

With extreme prejudice, Jamie thought. "Fine. But why is she even interested? This is the ice queen we're talking about."

"You will need to ask her yourself."

"What? Now you're holding back?"

"Each person has a secret place within them. I can see that place in the students and staff here, but it is not for me to share these things. I protect all students."

"But you tell me all these other things about them."

"These are things that they might share with others. There are some things they would never share with anyone. This is one of them."

"Fine. Can you at least let me know when they get together again?"

"Yes. When next they meet I will let you know."

"Awesome. Talk to you later." Jamie closed her cell phone, then noticed Abe still standing next to her. She'd been so caught up in the illusion of talking on the phone that she forget it was an illusion. After a discreet wave to the spirit, she turned and went back inside the school.

~

Justin shook his head. He and Sabrina stood by the trophy case at lunch. "No, sorry, she hasn't learned anything else. She said she had some false leads but didn't say what they were."

Jamie chose this moment to interrupt. "So, guys. Care to tell me what this is all about?"

The two looked over at Jamie in surprise. Justin looked trapped and caught, his eyes wide and mouth hanging open. Sabrina, on the other hand, only looked cold and hostile. Any guilt that Jamie might have seen on the cheer captain's face that morning was gone.

"H-hey, Jamie," Justin said. He glanced back and forth between Jamie and Sabrina and then backed away from them.

"You've caught me, Hattori," Sabrina said in a monotone. "What ever will I do?"

"How about you tell me what you're doing?"

"I'm trying to help you find out who the blogger is."

"Then why don't you just help me?" Jamie asked.

"I have a reputation to maintain. This reputation does not involve fraternizing with losers."

Jamie shook her head in confusion. "If I'm such a loser, why are you bothering to help?"

"It's in my best interest to make sure this gets dealt with. I don't want people to believe that they can drag my name through the mud."

Before Jamie could ask another question a girl called Sabrina's name from down the hall. Jamie turned to see Natalie, one of Sabrina's friends, running in their direction. Natalie skidded to a halt next to Sabrina and shoved her smart phone in the cheerleader's direction. Sabrina took a moment to puzzle out what she was being shown before her mouth opened and her eyes widened.

Jamie thought, for a moment, that Sabrina was about to lose her cool but whatever Sabrina was about to do was reined in tight and her face returned to its normal restrained expression. She tossed the phone to Jamie with carefully posed casualness. Jamie caught it and read the screen, which looked like the mobile version of 2thefairest.com.

"Have a look at what people will say about me to tear me down."

Sabrina Alvarez: Cheerleader Deep in the Closet

Most of you know Sabrina Alvarez as the homophobic Catholic captain of our cheer squad. But what few realize is that several years ago Sabrina was caught at summer camp locked in a romantic embrace with a fellow girl at camp. More details regarding this hypocrisy will be revealed over the next few days.

Jamie tossed the phone back to Natalie. "So you're saying that didn't happen."

"I'm saying that your lover Parker will do anything to break me. Remember that I've warned you."

"I'm pretty certain Parker's not the blogger."

"Keep telling yourself that," Sabrina said. "I'll make sure this stops if you can't do it."

Sabrina turned on her heel and stormed away, with Natalie trailing in her wake.

Parker said from behind Jamie, "Well, it's always good to see Sabrina leaving. What was that all about?"

Jamie turned to see Parker leaning against the trophy case, a smile on her face. Nearby stood Ashley, who waved when Jamie noticed her. "Someone's claiming that Sabrina had a lesbian experience at summer camp."

Parker's smile faded. "Oh?"

"Yeah, do you know anything about it?"

Parker looked down at her feet. "If I did, I couldn't say anything."

Jamie closed her eyes in dread. "Are you admitting to being the blogger?"

"What? No! I just know something about the incident."

"So there really was an incident?" Jamie asked, opening her eyes again and looking at Parker in surprise.

"Did it say who the other person was?" Parker asked.

"No... Wait, are you saying that you and Sabrina...?"

Parker stepped close to Jamie and put a shushing finger on Jamie's lips. "I told you, Sabrina and I share a secret. If she doesn't say anything, neither will I."

Jamie pulled Parker's hand aside. "If you know something, it will help us stop this."

Parker shook her head. "Look, I'm keeping my yap shut. If Sabrina wants to tell you about it, she can tell you about it. But I'm not saying a damn thing."

"I might be able to shed light and relieve Parker of her promise," Ashley said. Parker tensed and glared at Ashley. Ashley added, "It's not as big a secret as you think, Parker. After you left, everyone talked about you and Sabrina."

Raising a hand, Jamie said, "Okay, please, the half-communicating is driving me nuts. So Parker and Sabrina made out?"

Ashley nodded. "And they got caught by the counselors. Sabrina's parents flipped out and pulled Sabrina out of the camp. Parker was asked to leave as well to minimize outrage from other parents. The news leaked to the campers from the counselors, though. We talked about it for the rest of camp."

"So is Sabrina just ashamed of it?" Jamie asked.

Ashley shook her head. "She was put into a program to cure her of any gayness, just in case."

Jamie looked back at Parker. "This is your big secret? This is why Sabrina thought she had to warn me away from you?"

"Basically," Parker said, looking down at her shoes.

"We live in a city with a supervillain population, and Sabrina feels like she needs to warn me against one pushy lesbian?" Jamie asked. She slipped her hand into Parker's. "Right, well, I'm glad that's over. That was a false alarm I could have lived without. Let's hope that's the worst I have to deal with."

Parker leaned in and hugged Jamie, then poked her in the stomach. "You better believe I'm pushy."

CHAPTER 14 - WE NEED A BIGGER BOAT

Kensei ran rooftop to rooftop, sweat chill against her body in the icy wind. Her police scanner reported some sort of disturbance and screaming, so she made a beeline for that area. With Karl still incommunicado, Kensei found herself relying more and more on her scanner for information.

It had been almost a week without any further direct action from 2thefairest, but also no leads. As promised, the blogger had listed out the remaining details regarding Sabrina and Parker's brief fling as thirteen-year-olds at summer camp. But there had been no sign of *strixes* or any other traps. Kensei had begun to wonder if the goddess had lost interest in her.

And then a gorilla swung over the edge of the roof in front of her.

Kensei skidded to a halt, drew her sword and scrambled back a few steps. The gorilla seemed a bit bigger than she thought a gorilla would be, though that could have just been fear. He wore a blue and white singlet with a cargo belt around his waist, and a misty fog surrounded his fists. Kensei had read about the supervillain, Chillah Gorilla the Sub-Zero Simian Scientist, but she had gotten so used to big-name villains giving Karlsburg a pass that she had never had to deal with this sort of thing.

The supervillain roared, baring his long canines as the mist around his hands congealed into balls of ice that surrounded his fists. He charged Kensei, who jumped out of the way just as his fists hit the rooftop. The blow left holes through the tar paper and plywood of the roof.

Kensei rolled to the side and up onto her feet. Panic clouded her thoughts. This was not a mugger, this was four hundred pounds of angry muscle with the ability to create ice things! She turned and ran, only to have her feet slip from under her as she crashed into a sheet of ice that had not been there before.

As the ape raised his fists for another attack, Kensei slashed at the ape's feet with her katana. He roared in pain and stumbled back. This gave Kensei room to pull past the ice patch and get back up onto her feet. She backed slowly away from the gorilla, her katana at the ready. Her heels touched the edge of the roof. She didn't need to look back to see the long drop behind her.

This felt all wrong. Chillah Gorilla was a scientist. He usually had some elaborate scheme to rob government laboratories. He didn't just show up and smash things. Smashing things usually came later.

Chillah Gorilla charged. Kensei waited until the last second before leaping forward, planting her hand on the gorilla's hairy shoulder, and vaulting over him. At least, that was the plan. She got halfway into the air before the supervillain caught her ankle and threw her off of the roof.

She grabbed hold of a phone line with her free hand and jerked to a stop. Her arm felt like it wanted to leave its socket. The gorilla's hands were now free of ice. She wouldn't have thought he could thaw out his hands that fast. He ran back from the roof edge before turning and charging in her direction. He vaulted off the roof, his mighty bulk looming above her. Kensei cut the wire and let herself fall while she held onto one end.

The ape missed her by inches as she fell towards the street, then arced towards a shop window. She turned to plant her feet forward and crashed through the glass, shielding her eyes. Glass cut at her arms and legs just before she crashed through tables and chairs. Mariachi music filled the air. She looked around and realized she'd landed in Don Juan's Tacos. Patrons fled in terror from the destruction.

It took a couple tries for Kensei to push herself back onto her feet. She didn't know how badly she was bleeding, but she felt lightheaded. Bad sign. When her feet agreed to work with her, she picked up her sword and walked back to the front door. Broken glass crunched under her feet. No one stood nearby as she stepped out onto the sidewalk. Cobalt City had seen its share of supervillain attacks, so they knew not to stick around.

Chillah Gorilla landed in the middle of the street. The force of his impact caused the asphalt to cave in beneath him. He tensed himself to charge just as a golden light shot from the sky and blasted him backward. Kensei looked up to see a man surrounded by a golden nimbus of light descend from the sky under the power of rocket boots: Stardust.

"Everything alright here?" Stardust asked as he hovered over the ground.

Kensei nodded, her head feeling like it was about to wobble off.

Before Stardust could say anything else, his boots began making an unusual whining sound. Ice began to form around them and he drifted off uncontrollably just as Chillah Gorilla bounded back towards them and jumped onto Stardust. The ape had encased his fists in ice again and began to pummel at the superhero. The blows didn't get past his force field, but it was enough to keep Stardust from doing anything.

It felt like dragging her feet through molasses as Kensei lurched forward and built up to a run towards the two of them as they zigzagged down the street a few feet off the ground. Stardust raised a gauntlet to fire another blast at the Simian Scientist, but the ape encased that hand in ice as well. The blast shattered the ice but damaged the gauntlet in the process.

Kensei jumped on top of the gorilla, held onto the cargo belt, and slashed downward. The slash barely cut Chillah Gorilla, but it hurt the ape enough that he bucked back and tried to throw her off. She slashed again as she fell, but only managed to cut the canvas of the belt and fell to the asphalt again. The impact knocked the wind out of Kensei. She tried to move but felt a sickening grinding sensation in her chest.

A car rolled up next to her and a door opened.

"Are you okay?" a woman's voice asked.

Kensei looked up to see a gray-haired Asian woman, probably Chinese, standing above her. She wore khakis and a polo shirt. Kensei couldn't think of what to say.

"Do you have some healing factor that will help you get up again?" she asked.

Kensei shook her head.

"Alright, let me get you out of here."

The woman hooked her arms underneath Kensei's armpits and hauled her up into the car. Kensei struggled but she had no strength to resist. She wondered how much blood she had lost. She noticed numbly that a sheet lay over the seat, once white but now coverd in red-brown stains. Kensei wondered if it was dried blood just as she blacked out.

~

The world faded in by steps. First came the dull ache that spread through her body. Then the rhythmic beeping that matched her own heart. The antiseptic smell. And the feeling of rubber tubing resting against her arm. A lawn mower started up somewhere in the distance.

Jamie opened her eyes and looked around at the small hospital room. It seemed normal. Chair, IV, heart monitor, cheap painting of a vase of flowers on the wall. But something seemed off. Her gown seemed normal, complete with the open back. The walls were plaster with white paint. She glanced down at her wrist and noticed that she had no identification bracelet. She was about to try and call forth the spirit of the place but the door opened.

"Oh, good. You're awake." The woman from the night before entered with a bag from McDonald's and a steaming cup of coffee. "I brought you a little breakfast. Not sure if you drink coffee, but I'll drink it if you don't. I've also got a variety of other beverages if there's something specific you want."

"Who are you and where am I?"

"I'm Doctor Hao, and you're in my house in Morriston."

"What are you planning on doing with me?"

Doctor Hao smiled and laughed. "Well, I was planning on giving you time to eat breakfast. Then, if you'll let me, I was going to check out some of your stitches, give you some painkillers and put you in a cab to go home."

Jamie worked her jaw a bit more but could not get anything to make sense in her head.

The doctor moved the table around in front of Jamie on the bed and put her breakfast there. "I used to work in the emergency room. I'm now retired, but I offer my services to superheroes who land themselves into trouble and don't want their identity compromised. Jaccob gave me a call to tell me I'd be needed. I happened to be in Karlsburg when he called. Your costume has been laundered and patched, though I'd really recommend something a little hardier for the future. I'm assuming you would prefer to keep your real name a secret. What name would you like to be addressed by? I noticed the characters on your costume. Is that for Jiàn Sheng? Or Kensei? Maybe just Sword Saint?"

Jamie felt overwhelmed and fumbled at her bag of food in order to occupy her hands. "Kensei."

"A pleasure to meet you. I'm going to take care of some other stuff so you can eat your food in peace."

Once the doctor was gone, Jamie inspected the spirits of the food in the bag. While unhealthy, they weren't toxic. Once she felt safe, she inhaled the food and drank the coffee. As she started to feel more human, she panicked as she realized she didn't know how long she'd been there or what her mother must be thinking. She'd managed to stumble out of bed in a panic and remove half of the equipment hooked up to her by the time the doctor returned.

"Whoa, whoa, whoa... slow down there. What's wrong? Look, if you're worried about Chillah Gorilla, he's back at the Fermi Institute."

"My mom," Jamie said, staring at some of the wires that she tangled herself up in.

The doctor patiently helped untangle Jamie from the wires. "Is she held captive or in a death trap?"

Jamie paused and looked at Doctor Hao. "Um, no. She just hates superheroes and I was out late on a school night."

"Ah, one of Prather's 'Everymen?' Well then I think you're okay. You've only been here about five hours. The sun hasn't come up yet. Which was something I wanted to talk to you about."

Jamie sat down, still worried about blowing curfew but uncertain what to do about it.

"When I brought you back, you'd lost a lot of blood. You had cuts from the glass that needed stitches, a broken rib and several lacerations. You still have a lot of healing left to do, but you've done an unusual amount of healing in just five hours. Have you ever noticed that you heal fast? Or perhaps have damage resistance? You went through a plate glass window. You really should be cut up more than you were."

"No? I mean... I've gotten knocked around, but I just figured I'd gotten off lucky."

"Well, I didn't see anything strange about your blood. But I'd look into it. If you'll give me a minute, I'll check your injuries. You should be okay to go to school, though you'll be exhausted. No more tangling with super-gorillas. Doctor's orders. Then I can give you your costume and personal effects back. Was that your belt you had with you?"

Jamie shook her head.

The doctor helped Jamie undo her gown and go over the cuts and bruises. Doctor Hao talked as she worked. "Well, then I guess you've landed yourself a trophy. I'd probably get a professional to go over the gizmos that Chillah Gorilla had. Cobalt City is top ranked in accidental injuries from high tech gadgets. Mostly kids who find out about their parent's secret identities the hard way. The Keep used to offer that as a free service, but that was a different world back then. Oh, and you may want to rinse it out. I think the ape was keeping fruit in there as well."

Jamie closed her eyes. "You mean, like an apple?"

"Yeah, probably an apple. I didn't open any of it up. None of my business and I didn't know if it was booby trapped. But when the utility belt drips apple juice, it draws a bit of attention."

~

Jamie walked with awkward trepidation through the lobby of Starcom Tower. Five stories tall, with a giant flashing star on the floor in the middle of the room, it left Jamie feeling intimidated. Being a dark-skinned girl with dreadlocks and a ratty oversized sweatshirt while surrounded by white guys in shirts and ties didn't help her for first impressions. She walked up to the reception desk and waited for the receptionist to get off the phone.

Dr. Hao had been right: One of Chillah Gorilla's pouches had an apple in it. It had gotten smashed in the conflict, but *"Kallisti"* on the front was still legible. After a cab ride back to her lair, she had changed into her emergency set of clothes and spent the day freaking out over the fact that 2thefairest now had a supervillain on the payroll.

Over the course of the day, she dealt with the after effects of the night before. Parker had gotten a call from Jamie's mom at three in the morning, who accused Parker of lying when Parker claimed that Jamie was in the shower after a post-nookie slumber.

Sabrina, on the other hand, had looked at Jamie funny but then ignored her the rest of the day. And everyone talked about Stardust and some mysterious figure fighting it out with Chillah Gorilla in front of Don Juan's Tacos.

After school, she went back to her lair to grab some stuff before catching the bus downtown.

"Can I help you?" the Starcom receptionist asked. She reminded Jamie of an aging beauty queen.

"This is going to sound crazy, but would it be possible to see Jaccob Stevens?"

"Do you have an appointment?"

"No. I was just in the neighborh—"

"What is this regarding?"

"A private matter."

The receptionist handed Jamie a Starpad, Starcom's answer to the tablet computer, and said, "This has a questionnaire on it. Fill it out and your question will be dealt with in the order of severity. You can sit right over there while filling it out."

Jamie took her Starpad back to the seating area, where several other people sat with Starpads. They all looked a little rough for wear and avoided making eye contact with their peers. An air of sad desperation filled the area. She wondered how many of them were superheroes in over their heads. Jamie went back to the receptionist desk and set her Starpad on the edge.

"I'm sorry, before I dig in with this could you point me towards the ladies' room?"

After following some simple directions, Jamie holed up in one of the stalls and waited for a lull in the activity. When it seemed reasonably empty, she whispered, "Can I speak to the spirit of the tower?"

A golden knight appeared in front of her. He wore no helmet, but even the skin of his face was a glossy gold. "Yes?"

"I need to speak to Stardust."

"Mr. Stevens has a strict policy regarding visiting superheroes. You have already received the questionnaire. I encourage you to fill it out and return it to the receptionist."

"Please, this is an emergency. I'm in way over my head and need some sort of help or advice."

"There are many starting superheroes who feel overwhelmed by the challenges they face. Mr. Stevens' ability to be everywhere is still in development, and so he is obliged to filter requests for his help."

"Look, please. We had a team-up last night, so we've got some common ground. Plus, I have a utility belt filled with Chillah Gorilla's gadgets. I don't know what any of them do, but I don't think setting them off in the middle of a lobby would make you or Mr. Stevens very happy."

The spirit tilted his head, exasperated. "Extortion, is it?"

"I'm pretty serious about my desire to see Stardust."

"Very well. What do you want from me?"

"I want to get up to his office and speak to him. Since you know everything about this building, you can help me bypass security."

The spirit regarded her in silence for a moment before turning and walking through the stall door. "Follow me."

Jamie hurried after the spirit, who walked at a brisk pace back out to the lobby, across it to another set of back passages, and then to a nondescript elevator with a keypad next to it. Following his instructions, she entered a twenty-digit security code into the pad. After a moment, the elevator opened and she stepped inside to enter another twenty-digit code.

"This will take you straight up to Mr. Stevens' private office," the spirit said as it disappeared. "Good luck."

The doors opened and she faced an armored Stardust, with his gauntlets aimed at her. Their golden halo suggested that they were charged and ready to fire. "I suggest you talk really fast, Jamie Hattori."

Jamie dodged to the side of the elevator, out of sight from the outside. "I came looking for help."

"That's why I have questionnaires in the lobby. Is that not good enough for you?"

"I felt like my needs were too pressing. Someone sent Chillah Gorilla after me. I can't deal with that level of threat."

"Well, let me correct your first mistake: Chillah Gorilla appears to have had a bad reaction to his meds at the Fermi Institute. He didn't have a chance to get hired on."

"He was carrying an apple, enchanted to send him into a rage and home in on me."

"I think you need to come up with better lies."

"I have his cargo belt, which has the apple in it. That's the other reason I came here: I have a belt filled with evil genius thingies and I don't know what to do with it."

Jaccob sighed. "I hate magic. Fine, I'm powering down the gauntlets. Bring your evidence and let's hear the full story."

Jamie stepped gingerly out of the elevator. Jaccob's armor had dimmed some, but still held a golden aura. He led her down the hall to a conference room and offered her a seat. Sitting in a conference room in Starcom Tower was weird, but sitting across from a man in a glowing golden suit of powered armor was even stranger.

"How did you break in here? Nothing in your records indicates a computer background."

"You have records on me?"

"No, I just dug up all of your hospital and education records. Still running some cross-matching. But that's not answering my question.

"I asked the spirit of Starcom Tower to help me get up here."

"And he just rolled over for you?"

"Well, I did push him a bit."

Stardust glared at her for a bit and then shook his head. "Man. I *really* hate magic. Let's see this belt."

Jamie pulled the belt out of her bag and passed it to the superhero. He opened the sticky one first and pulled out the smooshed apple.

"*Kallisti*? To the fairest?"

Jamie nodded. "This all started a few weeks ago. Someone has been running a gossip blog called 2thefairest.com. It's mainly gossip about people in my high school. On the site is a golden apple, like that one. The site is heavily enchanted and can provoke irrational rage in targets and can steer them some. Not long after that, Louis Malenfant came up to me—"

"I'm sorry, did you say Louis Malenfant?"

"Yeah. He lives about six or seven blocks from me."

"And he just stopped by to say 'Hi?'"

"No, he's pretty steamed because I played ding-dong-ditch with him and a bunch of angry drug dealers and wants payback."

"You did what?"

"I was being chased by a bunch of drug dealers with guns. I couldn't take them all out, so I busted into Malenfant's house so that he'd deal with them. I figured he's some sort of dark god, so he could handle them. And he did. But now he's upset that Eris is in the neighborhood doing some sort of hoodoo."

"So you drew agg on them and then trained them onto the King in Yellow?" Stardust asked, eyes wide with disbelief.

"I don't know what any of that means."

"Never mind. Just… avoid Malenfant if you can. He's so much bad news it's ridiculous. And, uh, don't do drugs. Finish your story?"

Jamie had expected Stardust to be many things, but a huge dork was not one of them. "Louis Malenfant was upset because he believed Eris, the Greek goddess of discord, was meddling with things in Karlsburg. And from what I've seen, it seems like she's also behind the gossip blog. She's been using enchanted apples, like the one Chillah Gorilla had, to cause general problems. And I think she's turned students at my school into *strixes*."

"What's a '*strixes*?'"

"They're like vampire owl people."

Stardust laughed. "Are you saying the owls are not what they seem?"

"Maybe…?"

He shook his head. "Ahem. Never mind. Go ahead and finish."

"That's basically it. Until Chillah Gorilla got involved, I just figured this was solvable. But if she's got supervillains on her roster in some way then I think I'm screwed. I almost died fighting Chillah."

"Well, this should be easy. I reviewed the footage from the Fermi Institute of Mental Health. One of the orderlies helped Chillah escape. That orderly also had an apple like this. And footage shows that this apple was given to him by…" Stardust pointed at the wall, which turned into a freeze frame of footage outside of the Institute. "…Courtney Canvil. Missing student, parents brutally murdered. I think this is your goddess."

"Actually, I think she's just a minion. As best I can tell, she's a *strix*."

"Well, crap. Alright. If there's a vampire nest in the city that's something that needs to be dealt with. I can just track Courtney's cell phone back to where she's been hiding out and that will likely be where your goddess is lording over things…" His gaze seemed to focus on something else for a moment. "Hmm…"

"Hmmm?"

"Okay, it just sort of disappears. That's no problem. I can track her through… No, that's not working. Right, well, I can just crack open her blog and…"

"You might want to be careful with the blog. It's got, like, spells on it and stuff."

"Look," Stardust snapped, slamming a metal clad hand on the table. "I don't need some teenage jackass telling me how to do my job. First you break into Starcom Tower, then you start dragging your problems with a gossip queen across my desk like it's my problem. And now you try to critique my work?"

The glow around Stardust's armor intensified as he charged up his armor and gauntlets. Jamie didn't bother to argue with him and just ran out of the conference room. She cleared the door and rounded the corner just as a blast took out the door frame. Bits of plaster and wood sprayed towards her as she continued running down the hall.

The spirit of the tower appeared in front of her. "What did you do?!"

"This is not my fault," Jamie said. "I tried to warn him about the magic on the blog but did he listen? Nooooo…"

A blast struck the ground right behind Jamie and threw her forward. She slid headlong across the polished marble flooring, coming to a stop at a wall in a T-junction. She scrambled to her feet and ran down another hallway.

"Can I get some help here?" Jamie asked the spirit. "If Stardust kills me, my mom will never let me live it down."

"What can I do?" the spirit asked.

"You know this building inside and out. How can I get away from him until the spell wears off?"

"Fine, follow me!"

The spirit ran down the hall, and a heavy steel door opened and he gestured in there. She jumped through the door and it closed behind her. She heard muffled blasts and then Stardust yelling at someone. Jamie looked around to see locked storage units in the room.

"We've got a few seconds before he stops arguing with the A.I. and tries to just manually hack the system."

"Where are we?"

"The armory." One of the metal cabinets unlocked and began to disgorge something large and golden.

"What? Am I supposed to use the Wave Motion Gun against him or something? I don't want to shoot Stardust!"

"No, this is just the easiest and most replaceable way for you to get out of here."

The item that emerged from the locker looked like a motorcycle without wheels, glowing the same gold as Stardust's armor. A large door opened at the other end of the room. Wind whistled by, and a view of the city sprawled out in front of her.

"Is this some sort of hovercycle?"

"Yes. Mr. Stevens made a few of them after seeing one designed by Deathstar in Iteration 9615."

"I have no idea what any of that means."

"You don't have to. Just get on it and leave."

"That's your plan? Fly me out of here on hovercycle?"

The spirit nodded with a smile. "Yes."

"But he'll chase me!"

"That's the point. If he's attacking you out there, then he's not destroying the tower."

"You're an asshole! I don't even have a driver's license!"

"I have one job in this building and by God, I'm going to do it. You can stay here and wait for him or you can leave. Your call."

"I wish I could hit you." Jamie jumped on the hovercycle. "How does this work?"

"Power switch is on the left. Push forward on the handlebars to go down, pull back to go up. The lever on the left handle moves forward, the right hand lever pulls you backwards. So it works like a brake of sorts. I've already overwritten the security protocols for you so you're ready to go. The force field will activate once you get going and protect you some."

Jamie paused. "You're a spirit, you can't affect security protocols!"

The spirit shrugged and smiled.

"You are so lucky I can't hit you." She pulled out her just-in-case *tenugui* and wrapped it around her face. She didn't have a full costume, but at least there wouldn't be camera phones taking pictures of her face.

Kensei switched the bike on and it lifted up a few inches. She hit the accelerator and shot out of the tower like a bullet, then veered hard to the left to avoid the building across the street. She flew for a few blocks, wind barely blowing past her through the force field. She pulled back and rose up a ways until she could get her bearings. She put the river to her left and flew in the general direction of Karlsburg. She wondered if Agyo could counter-whammy 2thefairest's spell. She'd have to live that long to find out.

She was over Lafayette Park before the first blasts began to ricochet off of the force field. She looked back to see Stardust catching up with her. If she stayed up this high, he could just come up and punch her.

Kensei pushed forward and sent the bike into a dive. The ground loomed up hard, but she at least angled it so that she was following a street. She pulled up at the last minute. The undercarriage of the bike scraped along the asphalt and she clipped the top of a taxi before she gained control. She slowed the bike and turned down an alley. She hoped she could at least outmaneuver him.

And then he began raining down blasts from above her. The blasts bounced off the shield and hit the brick buildings on either side of her, raining debris and dust on her.

"Not fair!" Kensei screamed. She gunned forward out of the alley and turned onto the street. Cars veered around her and honked as she lowered down to street level. Any hopes that he might have stopped blasting her were thwarted when one of his blasts threw her to one side and the car next to her to the other.

She could only stare as the car bounced and rolled into the nearest building, her hands shaking on the controls of the bike. Was that what it was like for Grandpa Brown? His car tumbling and crumpling into a mess of twisted metal and broken glass? She had to stop this, and she had to stop it now. She was doing this all wrong. Musashi would have control of his environment, and she had lost all control of her environment.

She checked out her surroundings, spotted a sporting goods store, and began revising her plan. She aimed her bike for that and crashed through the front window. First stop: jump rope. She leaned over and snagged one off of a rack, tore it out of its packaging and tied a hasty knot around the accelerator while holding the reverse lever to keep it in place. She turned the bike towards the window and waited.

Stardust descended into view in front of the window and Kensei released the reverse thruster to allow the bike to rocket forward towards Stardust

"Banzai!" she screamed, waiting until the last moment to jump off. The bike hit Stardust square in the chest and launched him backwards.

Kensei ran back into the store to obtain her next piece of equipment: an aluminum baseball bat. She hurried to the back door and waited. Stardust flew back into the store and she ducked out the door, the emergency alarm screaming as she did so. In the alley behind the store, she positioned herself out of sight.

Stardust came through the door and stopped to look around. Kensei used this moment to swing the bat at his legs. He was hovering over the ground, so she knew it wouldn't trip him. But since he relied on his boot jets, it would at least destabilize him. Her human strength with a baseball bat wouldn't penetrate his force field, but up close she could at least control the fight. Swatting at his hands with the bat would keep him from blasting her and hitting his legs would diminish his control over flight.

After a minute of this, as Kensei's arms felt like they were about to fall off from exhaustion, Stardust yelled, "Okay, okay... I think I'm okay. The spell is wearing off."

Kensei stepped back, bat still at the ready. Stardust powered down and lowered himself to the ground. "So, you were saying something about there being magic spells on the site."

Kensei nodded. She noticed that a crowd had gathered at the alleyway.

"I think I figured that out the hard way. Sorry about that. You should get going, um... What's your name in the mask?"

"Kensei."

"Right, Kensei. You should get going. I need to do some damage control."

A man from the crowd yelled, "Stardust, can we get a picture of you two together?"

Stardust shrugged and looked at Kensei. She shook her head and moved to stand next to Stardust and held up two fingers in victory. "*Yatta.*"

CHAPTER 15 - LEGACIES

It was raining buckets when she got home, with thunder and lightning filling the sky. The storm had a sense of doom about it, like it heralded the end of the world.

Something about her house felt odd when Jamie walked in the door. Nothing looked out of place, but an air of emptiness filled the home. Her parents were usually home by now. Her dad should be cooking dinner and her mom should be settling in for tonight's episode of *Lyle Prather Live*. But the house was silent.

"Hello?" Jamie called out.

She heard movement and then her dad poked his head out of his study. "Oh, you're home. Glad you're okay. I was thinking pizza for dinner, but wanted to wait for you to get home before ordering."

"What's going on?"

Charles thought for a moment and then said, "You made the front page of the *Gazette*. And Lyle Prather's blog."

Her dad disappeared back into his study and came back with a framed newspaper clipping. It showed an action shot of her as Kensei on Chillah Gorilla's back, katana raised high, while the ape pounded on Stardust.

"You framed it?" Jamie asked. She felt dizzy with shock. "What if Mom sees it?"

"She's already seen it. That's why she's not here. I don't know what her long-term plan is, but suffice to say it was a long night of arguing and she took some things and left."

Jamie dropped down to sit on the floor. She covered her face with her hands and tried to make sense of what was going on.

Her dad sat down next to her. "The lion design on the hand guard of the katana's pretty unique. And whoever took the picture got a good shot of it. Once you identify the katana, you can kinda tell it's you in the costume. It appeared on Prather's site almost right away. And then your mom went nuts. At that point she wouldn't believe that I hadn't put you up to being a superhero."

She felt a sob bubble up. "Why would she blame you?"

Charles wrapped an arm around Jamie's shoulders. "Um, because when your mother and I met, I used to run around in a mask and swing a katana as I beat up criminals. Just like my father did. And his father. And countless generations before them. And until Grandpa Brown died, we had been preparing you to take my place someday. But when your mother got involved with the Everymen, I agreed to hang up the mask and get you out of martial arts and stuff. Neither of us really expected you to do it on your own."

Everything clicked in Jamie's head. The arguments. The suspicion .Why her parents had put her into the sports they did. Why her dad was so cool with her doing all this against her mom's wishes. Jamie doubled over and began to sob uncontrollably and her dad held her tighter.

When she settled down, her dad moved her to the couch and called in the pizza. He came back and they sat together for a while.

"What was your name when you were a superhero?" Jamie asked, breaking the silence.

"Hanzo."

Jamie scrunched up her face. "Really?"

Her dad frowned in confusion. "Yeah. Is something wrong with that?"

"Like Hattori Hanzo?"

"Yes…"

"That's a ridiculous secret identity."

"It was the traditional name our family used…"

"It's also ridiculously obvious! I mean… the only thing I can think of that would be dumber would be if Wild Kat's secret identity was actually something like… Kathy Wild."

"If I'm so dumb, I guess you don't want to see the picture I have of me and Huntsman…"

Jamie slouched back into the couch in mock defeat. "Well, fine... I guess it's not that lame."

Her father laughed and she joined in, though it felt almost like sobs. As the laughter died away, the silence crept back in. The pizza arrived, and food helped her mood even if she continued to feel hollow. They sat without talking for a good long while, listening to the storm rage outside.

"Did you try to stop her from leaving?" Jamie asked, breaking the silence.

"Yes. Did you think I wouldn't?"

"You just seem so happy about the situation."

"I don't know that 'happy' is the word I'd use." Her dad sighed.

"Why doesn't this bother you more?"

"I've had all day to deal with this on my own. And while I love your mother, it was also hard living a lie. I couldn't support her fanaticism. Besides, I miss the lifestyle, and I want to be able to support you."

Before Jamie could say anything, someone banged on the door.

Her dad leaned back across the couch and looked out the window. "Looks like Parker. And someone else."

Jamie pulled herself up and shuffled towards the door. She was happy that Parker had stopped by, but she wasn't really in the mood for going out somewhere. She thought of suggesting that Parker come in and hang out, but wasn't sure how her dad would react to that.

In the porch light, Jamie could see that Parker stood waiting with Cleopatra Thunder, who looked damp and annoyed. Parker waved manically with a nervous smile on her face.

Cleo said, "You're Jamie, right?"

Jamie nodded.

"My dad wants to talk to you. Sent me to come get you. I thought having Parker here would make things easier."

"Why does your dad want to see me?"

"I can't say I understand why he wants to do anything. He gave me this envelope to give to you in case you were uncertain."

It was a letter-sized envelope, sealed, with "Jamie" scrawled across the front. She tore it open and pulled out a note written on the back of a grocery store receipt. "Stardust called me up out of the blue to tell me I should help you. If you don't get over here right now I will come get you myself. P.S. Don't show this to my daughter Tera."

"Are you coming with me or not?" Cleopatra asked.

Jamie nodded and stuffed the note in her pocket. "Dad? I need to go. Something's come up."

~

Cleopatra's father, Cole Washington, lived in a rough part of West Key a mile from Bifrost. He stood on the front porch watching the rain from the shelter of the awning. Cleopatra was out of Glenda before the car had come to a complete stop, and she strode up to her father while Parker turned off the engine.

"Okay, so I brought Jamie here. Want to tell me what's going on?"

"Nope. How about you wait out here with your derby kid, Tera? I want to talk to this girl in private."

"Damn it, Dad!" Thunder rolled as lightning struck the street down the block. Jamie jumped at the nearness of the strike.

"Don't take that tone with me, Tera, or I'll send you home and I'll drive Jamie back myself. Or am I not allowed to drive my own damn car?"

Cleo glared at her father but went and sat on one of the wooden chairs on the porch. Parker joined her while Jamie followed Cole into the house. Parker waved nervously to Jamie, and Jamie returned the wave.

Inside, the house smelled like old man. Piles of newspaper lay stacked up around the living room, as well as piles of dirty dishes. He continued back into the kitchen, stopped to pull a box from the freezer, and then walked out the back door and stood on the back porch. The backyard was a similar disaster, overgrown with weeds. Some tires lurked in the tall grass around an old rusted swing set.

Up close, she could see that scars covered his face. He glanced conspiratorially towards the front of the house while opening up the box from the freezer. Inside were a dozen or so powdered mini-doughnuts.

"Alright, I don't think Tera can hear us from here." He turned back towards Jamie as he fished out a doughnut and asked, "So, you're supposed to be a superhero?"

"Um, yes?" Jamie said. She didn't know what to make of all this, or how this old man knew Stardust. She waved off the box when he offered it.

"So, I was just about to have some dinner when some bicycle courier showed up here. I didn't know they came here, but sure enough, some half-naked girl wearing a bicycle helmet shows up and delivers a package to me. I open it to find some cell phone. Soon as the girl left, the phone rings. You know who it was? Jaccob Stevens. Can you beat that? Said he had a young hero with a magical problem she was dealing with and he needed someone with that sort of experience. I don't know how deep he had to dig to track me down, but he sure as hell did."

Jamie just stared at this strange man, afraid to speak. He popped a doughnut into his mouth in one bite and barely chewed before swallowing.

"So you wear a mask and claim to be Kensei, huh?"

Jamie nodded.

"I did that gig a long time ago. My name was Midnight Thunder. It seemed less cliché at the time. You got any powers?"

"Yeah. I can see spirits. And talk to them."

"A shaman then?"

Jamie screwed up her face, imagining herself wearing beads and feathers and dancing around a fire. "I don't know that I'd call it that."

"Oh, I've met a few of you. And you all had some sort of fancy name for it. There was a voodoo houngan, a Shinto priest, a Baptist gal who thought her spirits were all angels. Oh, she was a foxy lady. But the end story is that you do all sorts of weird stuff with animistic spirits."

Jamie shrugged. "Sure."

"So what's the magical problem you're dealing with?"

"Well, it started with this blog—"

"I'm not interested in the whole shebang. Just give me the *Reader's Digest Condensed.*"

"The goddess Eris is trying to kill me. I think."

Cole nodded. "Yeah, I know a good deal about gods. I don't know if you can tell, but I used to be a god."

Jamie focused on the spiritual level around Cole. Something lingered there, but she couldn't tell what. She shrugged. "Not really."

Cole sighed. "Guess it doesn't matter now. But believe it or not, I used to be the Norse god Thor."

"Aren't you a little black to be a Viking?"

He laughed and popped another doughnut. "That's the first thing you need to learn. The avatars and incarnations of the gods don't have to look a damn thing like the gods themselves. They don't even have to be the same gender. It's the spirit of the person that matters. You look like you know how to fight. That so?"

Jamie nodded.

Cole stepped into the kitchen, put the box back in the freezer, then walked out into the mud and overgrown weeds in the backyard. If the rain bothered him, he didn't show it. But then, if he'd been the Norse storm god, maybe he was used to it.

"C'mon," Cole said. "Let's see what you've got."

Jamie looked at the downpour and frowned. "Are you serious?"

"What, afraid of a little rain? You don't always get to fight in pleasant weather."

"No, I'm afraid of breaking you since you're all... old and fat."

Jamie walked out into the wind and was instantly soaked in the cold, wet rain. Her feet sank into mud up to her ankles. She tried to size up Cole as she walked. He moved slow and stiff, but that could be a ruse. His layers of fat could hide muscle. And what sort of effect did having a god in you have on your body? The rain and mud would be the biggest liability. She relied on speed and agility, but this would slow her down and cause her to slip.

Cole raised his fists like a boxer and smiled. Jamie settled into an aikido stance, hands open and loose in front of her. She'd hoped he would make the first attack, but he just stood there and waited, his smile growing broader.

She feinted in with a chop, intending to get him to raise his arm in defense and give her an opening to throw him. He did raise his arm, but when she shifted to grip his forearm, he swung back and sent her flying. She rolled through the mud but came back up on her feet.

Cole just shook his head and smiled. Jamie clenched her fists and came in with a different style. She swung her fists but he mostly just blocked and dodged to the inside of her punches. She tried for a kick but pulling her foot from the mud weakened the force. Cole shifted his weight and then lurched down awkwardly and clutched at his thigh.

Jamie stopped and leaned forward. "Are you alr—"

Cole used that moment to deliver an uppercut that caught Jamie square on the jaw. Jamie felt her feet leave the ground as motes of light swam in her vision. Something hit the small of her back and she fell with it to the ground. She landed hard and struggled to breathe. When she sat up, Cole stood there with his fists up again. Jamie shook her head and pulled herself back to her feet. Looking around she saw that she had hit the top of the swing set, which now lay in pieces around and under her.

She considered the old man and realized that she could use the terrain to her advantage. She ran towards him, fists clenched and trying to look like she meant to just pound away at him again. He frowned in confusion and then she dropped and slid through the mud between his legs. Once clear on the other side, she rose up and punched him repeatedly in the kidneys. He tried to turn and maintain his stance but she could circle him fast enough from behind that he couldn't quite get to her.

Finally he bolted forward and tried to turn while he had distance. She ran to catch up and climbed his back and punched him in the ear a few times until he grabbed her by the back of the hoodie, pulled her over his head and slammed her face-first into the ground. She pushed herself up, spitting mud.

"You had enough yet?" Cole asked.

Jamie shook her head.

Cole smiled and raised his fists.

Jamie came in with the open-handed stance again and went with the same feint. But this time, when Cole raised his arm, she pulled herself up onto it instead of going for a throw and launched herself over his head to land behind him. He turned before she could punch him in the back again, but she managed to sock him in the face before he got his guard up. Without grace, he just grabbed her by the front of her sweatshirt, lifted her off the ground, and threw her down again.

As her eyes regained the ability to focus, she made eye contact with Cole and abruptly found herself falling.

And then she stood in hip-deep water off of a rocky coast, her body jolted like she had woken from a dream of falling just before hitting the ground. Wind tore at her, and a wave knocked her forward onto the rocks before trying to pull her back into the ocean. She held onto the rocks for dear life and felt her fingernails tear. Then a great toothy maw grabbed her by the shoulder and pulled her further inland.

She looked around and had no idea where she was. The area smelled of rain, salt, and rotting seaweed. Behind her, the land disappeared into a thick forest of pine and spruce trees. Her clothing had changed: sweatshirt, jeans, and sneakers replaced with a yellow *kimono*, red *hakama*, and a pair of *tabi*. Her katana had been thrust through her *obi*.

A glance around and she saw the source of her salvation: A golden-furred lion with a thick red mane. The lion looked like a regular lion, but somehow *wrong*. It reminded her a little of the *shishi* temple guardians that came up in Japan, a few iterations removed from the original Indian statues of the Asiatic lion. Its head was a little too wide, and it had red tufts of fur around its paws.

The lion watched her for a moment before saying in a deep booming voice, "You really shouldn't be here."

A memory came to her of this lion, standing by her side as she stood over Alexis Sohda, who lay in a pool of blood while something dark and awful loomed over her. Then, as now, she screamed...

...and found herself back in the rain, with Parker leaning over her and stroking her face. Parker's eyes were red-rimmed and wild.

"What...?"

Parker sobbed and hugged Jamie. "Oh, thank god. Thank god, thank god, thank god."

Jamie hugged back. "What happened?"

"I was going to ask you that. We heard you screaming and came to find Cleo's dad crouched over you and sort of frozen while you just screamed and screamed and screamed. What the hell happened?"

Jamie shook her head. "We were sparring. And then... then I just blacked out." She mentally added another lie to the pile she'd already told to Parker.

Cleopatra yelled, "What the hell were you thinking? What on earth prompted you to try and spar with a teenage girl young enough to be your granddaughter?"

Cole spoke in softer, soothing tones, but Cleopatra just kept yelling. "You had a heart attack! Do I need to remind you of this? You need to take your medicine and not do something stupid like get into a fight in the middle of a rainstorm. Wait, is that powdered sugar on your lips? Do you have another stash of those stupid doughnuts?"

Parker helped Jamie up just as Cleopatra stormed off around the house. If Cole had said something to really set her off, Jamie didn't hear it. A moment later, Jamie heard a car start and drive off. Back under the shelter of the porch, Jamie slumped to the wooden floor. Cole stumped up.

He glanced at Parker and then looked pointedly at Jamie. Jamie just shook her head to the unasked question. "I want to talk to you more and show you some things. Bifrost closes at 9 PM tomorrow. Think you can come by?"

Jamie hesitated. "Maybe."

"I could give you a ride," Parker said.

"You won't be able to join me when I go in," Jamie said.

Parker frowned and shrugged. "I can deal."

~

Jamie stumbled in the door and waved to her dad, who opened his mouth to speak but froze when he saw the thick coating of mud. She held up a finger to indicate she'd have the conversation with him later. Her phone rang as she put her foot on the first step to the stairs. She needed out of the clothes she was wearing and to use all the hot water in her shower, so she ignored it.

But instead of going to voicemail, it just continued ringing. At the top of the stairs, she pulled the phone out and looked at the caller ID. It said: "This is Jaccob Stevens. Answer your phone."

She answered. "How did you get my number?"

"I own the largest telecommunications company in the world. How do you think I got your number?"

"Good point. What's up?"

"I need you to suit up and meet a couple masks over at the rooftop above E-Z Klean Laundry in an hour."

Jamie thought for a moment. That was a block away from her lair.

As if reading her mind, Stardust said, "Yes, it's right next to your lair."

"How do you know that?"

"Your cell phone allows me to track you. You really should turn it off or leave it at home when you're going to be doing something secret. You should also talk to the owner of the property you're squatting in so that he knows you're squatting there."

"It's an abandoned bolt hole that someone named Devil Cat used decades ago. He's retired."

"Yes, but the property it's built into is currently owned by an acquaintance of mine. I should see how he'd like me to handle this."

"Who's the owner?"

"I'm not sure how he wants to be identified."

"Can you be more cryptic?"

"Yes. I could say, 'The moose wants his lager inspected' but it would convey absolutely no information."

"Fine, can I have an hour and a half? I have mud in places I didn't know were places and need to shower."

"Do I want to know why you have mud in all those places?"

"Your friend Cole wanted to test my kung fu."

"He's less of a friend and more of a 'closest I could find to a magical superhero in Cobalt City on short notice.' I didn't see anything about kung fu in your file."

"You have a file on me?" Jamie asked. Her dad poked his head around and looked up at her from the bottom of the stairs with a confused look on his face. She waved him away. "You met me this afternoon, how do you have a file on me?"

"Have you met me? Between me and my A.I., I can obtain all sorts of information."

"Fine. Whatever. I'll meet your friends in an hour and a half." She hung up without waiting for him to respond.

"What was that about?" her dad asked.

"Stardust is a nosy jerk who has arranged a playdate for me with other superheroes."

"That's good, right?"

Jamie shook her head. "I don't know. I'll tell you after I've had a long hot shower and met with these people."

~

Kensei crouched on the rooftop of E-Z Klean Laundry, listening to her police scanner. She'd tried to get ahold of Karl to no effect, so she sat and brooded over what to do about that. She was jolted from her reverie by someone tapping her shoulder. She jerked forward, drawing her sword and bringing it in line with whatever assailant had snuck up on her.

Her opponent didn't flinch as he regarded the sword in his face. Instead, he examined the blade. "Very nice. Sengoku period, yes?"

Kensei nodded, slowly realizing who stood in front of her. She'd grown up watching him on the news with other members of the Protectorate. His hunter green hooded cloak, golden chainmail shirt, bow, and quiver together formed an iconic image of Cobalt City dating back to the American Revolution. No one knew just how many men had worn the mantle of Huntsman over the years.

"The sword looks familiar, especially the hand guard. Are you any relation to Hanzo?"

She nodded again. This incarnation of Huntsman seemed young, though still older than Kensei. She couldn't make out his face in the shadows of his hood, but then realized he wore a cowl mask underneath. She hastily put her sword away and gasped, "OhmygodImsosorry."

"It's fine, Kensei," he said, with a hint of a smile on his face that belied his matter-of-fact tone. "I did opt to mess with you a little bit. A little levity when you're starting out can be good."

"You're one to talk, Huntsman," said a woman's voice.

Kensei looked up to see another Cobalt City legacy that had seen a few incarnations: Libertine. She hovered a few feet above Huntsman (*hovered!*), her crimson cloak billowing about in the wind. She dressed in men's clothing from the nineteenth century: a crimson jacket with golden embroidery over a gold-embroidered vest, golden trousers, white hose and black leather shoes. A golden mask concealed her face with an elaborate pattern of whirls that suggested leaves and flower petals, with diamonds and pearls spread across the surface.

Never before had Kensei felt so shabby in her costume.

As she floated down to the rooftop, Libertine said, "Tell her what you did for fun last night."

"I reviewed and cataloged all instances that past Huntsmen have reported regarding pirate ghosts. The files were a mess. And then I did some archery drills to try and work out some kinks."

"I rest my case."

"Not everyone works so hard to earn the name 'Libertine.' Besides, I let you take me to roller derby."

"You like roller derby?" Kensei asked, surprised. She was willing to latch onto anything that kept her from jumping up and down and clapping her hands in fangirl glee.

Huntsman frowned in thought. "It was enjoyable."

"My, um, girlfriend plays junior roller derby. I mean, my friend. Who's a girl. That I kiss sometimes. Not that there's anything wrong with that. Or that you would think that there was anything wrong with that. I'm babbling aren't I?"

Huntsman and Libertine both nodded.

"Perhaps we can go to a bout together if we ever get to the secret identity stage of our friendship," Libertine said. "We can double date."

Huntsman cocked his head at Libertine, then shook his head. "Let's talk about vampires. Other Huntsmen and I have dealt with vampires over the years."

Kensei had a flash of geeking out. Before she could stop herself she said, "Like in 1972 with Doctor Shadow? Or in 2006 when Huntsman and Velvet took on a vampire nest in the Hollows?"

Huntsman opened his mouth, closed it, then said, "Yes. Among others. So Stardust came to me with the possibility of a new vampire nest in Cobalt City."

"He doesn't handle this sort of thing himself?" Kensei asked.

"Hunting vampires is subtle and precise work. He's neither. But that's a different topic. One of the kids you took out is still in lock up. I guess his mother wasn't willing to vouch for him."

"How do you know which kids were arrested? Wait, is this another example of Stardust knowing everything?"

"Basically. If you ever decide to buy him a Christmas present, make sure you use cash and buy it somewhere really obscure. Anyway, Travis Lambros tests negative for the vampiric virus. But there are plenty of other things out there that fit the profile for 'vampire,' so that's not conclusive. Just less inclined to mean an epidemic that can only be solved with fire and stakes through the heart."

"He's also surprisingly resistant to psychic probes and conventional interrogation techniques when it comes to the identity of his boss," Libertine said. "I'm thinking it must be a magical compulsion. I can find out who his crush was in first grade but the identity of his boss is like a minefield filled with magical booby traps."

"Right. So I'm thinking we could patrol the area, see if we can find any *strixes* skulking about. Then we run them to ground and find out where their base of operations is."

"Sounds like a great plan," Kensei said.

The other two superheroes looked at her expectantly.

Kensei looked over her shoulder, in case she was missing something behind her, then touched the front of her mask. "Do I have something on my face?"

"We were hoping you could show us around," Huntsman said. "Since you're the local expert."

"So, wait… you want *me* to patrol with *you*?"

Huntsman turned to Libertine. "When did I reach the point where people freaked out when I wanted to team up with them?"

"I think it was one of the incarnations of the Huntsman from the early 1800s."

"What? No. I mean me, specifically."

"Maybe when you became old enough to drink?"

Huntsman looked at her for a moment and then looked over at Kensei. "Okay. So let's go find some *strixes*."

CHAPTER 16 - KEEPING SECRETS

Parker pulled into a spot in the parking lot for Bifrost Roller Rink and set her emergency brake. "Sure I can't come in with you?"

Jamie frowned, frustrated that Parker had reneged on her offer to respect her privacy. "Yeah, I'm sure."

"But, but, but... But that's not fair. We're dating. And going to Homecoming together. I tell you everything!"

"Except about Sabrina."

"That's different. That was a sworn secret. There was a pinkie promise and everything."

"And this is something private for me. Can you respect that?"

"But I tell you everything else. I tell you about the stench of my derby gear, my poop, weird arguments my moms have."

"I don't want to know about those things. And, really, I wish you'd stop."

"But my life is an open book to you! When there's corn in the toilet, I tell you!"

"You act as though no one ever tells you 'No.'"

"People tell me 'No.' It doesn't happen often, because I pitch an awesome fit. But it happens. I think last year my step-mom told me no."

Jamie opted to cut this off before it went further. She hated that her secret identity was already screwing up her very confusing first relationship. She leaned over and kissed Parker on the cheek before she opened the door and got out. "Pitch away."

"But I gave you a ride here!"

"You offered. I was willing to figure out my own ride over here, but you insisted, even knowing you couldn't come in."

"I thought that was a ruse and that you'd tell me in the car."

"Maybe later I'll let you know what this is about."

Parker leaned over and slammed the door shut before pulling back out of the spot and speeding off into the night. Jamie watched her go, wondering if it was right to keep Kensei from Parker. When Parker was out of sight, Jamie turned towards the rink.

Patrolling with Huntsman and Libertine had been an unusual experience. They hadn't found any *strixes*, but Libertine had guided them to several muggings, break-ins, and assaults just as they were happening. Jamie didn't think Karlsburg had ever been that crime-free, even when Karl had been guiding her to crimes.

Huntsman came up with some tactics to best use their combined skill sets. On some occasions, Kensei went in alone while Huntsman and Libertine watched. And after every crime in progress they stopped, the two older superheroes offered feedback. She couldn't decide if they had been training her or testing her. If it was the latter, she wasn't sure if she passed.

Jamie banged on the door to Bifrost. After a few minutes, Cole came up and let her in. He practically bounced as he led her back into the rink. He'd set up a heavy bag on one of the lower parts of the ceiling.

Jamie raised her eyebrows. "I thought this was supposed to be you teaching me about gods."

"It is. Trust me. Warm up on that thing while I talk."

Jamie shrugged and stretched before beginning light punch and kick drills on the heavy bag.

"Right. So, gods. When I became the avatar of Thor, I spent a lot of time learning what I could about how gods worked. I met sorcerers, shamans, other gods. I don't think I'm an expert, but I know a damn sight more than most people in these cities. Especially with Doctor Shadow gone.

"The word 'god' is a nebulous term that gets thrown around a lot without a lot of clear definition. On one end of the spectrum you have spirits. You might have household gods that watch over your house, but they're ultimately just the animistic energy of your house given shape by the beliefs of the people in the house."

"Yeah, I'm familiar with those." Jamie worked up the intensity of her drills, settling into a good groove. If nothing else, the warm-up loosened some of the tension out of her shoulders.

"On the other end of the spectrum are the singular entities. You live in Karlsburg, right? You know Louis Malenfant?"

Jamie nodded.

"He's the avatar of the King of Yellow, the embodiment of madness. To call him a god implies that he has worshippers or desires worship. The King in Yellow is simply madness. And in all the many universes that exist, there is only one of him."

"Thank goodness for small favors."

"And, in between, there are gods like Thor and Eris. They come out of cultures. Instead of just a single spirit of a storm, you now have an entity that embodies all storms like Thor or Zeus. But this is not to be confused with whatever entity exists in the Coil that embodies the raw essence of 'Storm.'"

"What's the Coil?"

"Picture a big spring, but instead of a coil of wire, it's a bunch of universes stacked end to end in a tight spiral. Parallel earths. Alternate universes. That's the Coil."

"And you just travel between them all the time?"

"Only a couple times. Mostly I know about it from Doctor Shadow."

"Right."

"Gods are very culture specific, too. The Norse Thor is not the same as the German Donar, though they arose from the same place. The Greek Eris is not the same as the Roman Discordia. They also rely on human belief. Or at least awareness. Even if you don't actively worship Thor, enough people are aware of him that they imagine him as being someone. There are gods that have disappeared from the world because they disappeared from human memory."

Jamie nodded, the heavy bag rocking from the impact of her blows. It felt good to get all this energy out of her system.

"Look at your hands," Cole said.

Jamie paused and looked over in confusion. "Huh?"

"Look down at your hands. Not the skin, look at the spirits there."

Jamie did and didn't see anything right away. With strain, she could make out some motion on the spiritual level. She took a deep breath to clear her mind and pushed harder.

And then she saw them.

Swarming around and through her hands were spirits, so tiny they were almost mindless. Spirits of the air, which were usually so ephemeral that she just ignored them, were the first she saw. It took her a while to recognize other spirits: motion, blood, skin, bone. She didn't even know there were spirits for these things, but as she saw them swimming through her hands she knew instantly what they were.

Cole said, "I'm not proud to say it, but I've fought a lot of women in my life. Some of the most vicious non-powered female assassins you've ever seen. You hit harder than they did, and you take a hit better than they did. I've known other shamans who have controlled spirits to help them in fights. I'm guessing you've been controlling them subconsciously without realizing it. The harder you have to try in a fight, the more you call on them."

Jamie wondered now if this was what Dr. Hao noticed indirectly. Had she reflexively protected herself from the worst of her injuries through spirits? Or healed faster because of it?

"Once you know how to consciously control them, you can learn to do other things. I've seen shamans convince the spirit of a house to let them pass through a wall, spirits of wind to carry them, or spirits of stone to create walls."

The spirits slowly began to fade from her view. The wind spirits drifted away into the air, spirits of blood and bone absorbed back into her body. With effort she could slow them down in their departure, but they slipped away despite her best efforts.

"So I can answer your questions about gods as needed, but I also figure if you're going to be facing any sort of god you'll want to know how to use your powers to your full limit. Now that you know you can pull spirits in to affect the physical world, you can try to do it consciously. That's what I want you to focus on today."

"Okay, before we get started, can I ask questions?"

"Sure, shoot."

"2thefairest has two main tricks she's been using that I hoped you could explain. The first is that she seems to be about planting apples that have some sort of spell in them that causes people to go a little nuts."

"An avatar can turn a mundane object into one of their divine tools. When I was Midnight Thunder, I could turn any club or hammer into Thor's hammer Mjölnir."

"So 2thefairest can turn any apple into the Apple of Discord. Okay, then how about the *strixes*? She's been turning people into these sort of vampire owls from Greek myth."

Cole nodded. "Gods can also bring lesser creatures from their pantheon over and make people into avatars. I haven't seen strixes, but I've seen trolls, Valkyries, hopping ghosts, and nagas, just to name a few. They still look human, but they gain abilities based off of the creature possessing them."

"Can they be cured?"

"The spirit riding them can be destroyed and cast back to their native realm if you have a weapon that can affect spiritual things. I took out a lot of these avatars with Mjölnir."

"Okay, so what is an avatar anyway?"

"It's one of two ways a god can appear in the mortal world. It can connect to a mortal host and imbue them with power."

"Like a parasite?"

Cole arched an eyebrow. "I guess you could describe it that way."

"It's something Malenfant said. He said that he was nothing like a 'memetic parasite.' Whatever that means."

"I guess he'd say that, wouldn't he?"

Jamie shrugged. "So what's the other way?"

"Incarnating. They can create a body for themselves out of nothing. They can control an incarnation more directly than an avatar, but it has no mortal identity to fall back on. An incarnation has to build up any resources in the material world from scratch."

Jamie nodded.

"Any other questions? No? Good." Cole went back in the office and came out with a desk lamp. He plugged it in and turned it on, then angled the light towards Jamie.

Wincing in the glare of the light, Jamie said, "Agh, is that necessary?"

"I think annoyance will help. I want you to contact the spirit of the light bulb and convince it to shut off."

"Are you kidding me?"

"Nope. Get going."

Jamie concentrated and could sense, but not quite see, the spirit of the light bulb. She tried to will it closer to her, but just felt like it pulled back.

"Hello, spirit of the light bulb?" she asked.

"Hi! Hi! How are you!?" the spirit answered.

"I'm doing great. Could you do me a favor?"

"I might! I like to be helpful! Do you need light?!"

"No, I actually need you to turn off." Jamie said, smiling a bit.

"Okay!"

Jamie felt shocked and relieved. "Really?"

"Sure! If you can make the electricity stop running around in me, then I can turn off!"

"How can I do that?" Jamie asked.

"There's a switch! You flip the switch and I turn off!"

Jamie rolled her head back and groaned. "I don't think this is going anywhere."

"Then this is going to be a long couple hours for you," Cole said.

Jamie strained to sense the electricity spirit in the lamp. "Hello, electricity spirit?"

"yesimherehowareyouthingsareverybusyinhere"

"Can you perhaps stop going through the lamp?"

"nononononohavetokeepupwattagekeepupwattage"

"Okay, I think I preferred the light bulb. Light bulb?"

"Yes!"

"Electricity isn't wanting to stop. How about you just turn yourself off?"

"No! The switch! I can't stop the current! There are rules! I must follow the rules!"

Jamie could feel a headache building between her eyes. She kept trying to argue with the light bulb spirit but the spirit wouldn't budge. She never knew that light bulbs could be such sticklers for law and order. Cole left her alone to work elsewhere in the rink while she worked at this.

After twenty minutes of getting nowhere with the light bulb, Cole returned and looked at the lamp. "It's still on."

"I know it's still on," Jamie snapped.

"Some shamans I've known have used some sort of focus to make it easier. Some had an item, others prayed or sang. One person spoke in Latin. Usually it was something that had significance to them."

Jamie frowned and looked at the light. She'd left her sword at her lair, so that couldn't help her right this moment. And she didn't want to just give up. The only language she knew how to speak besides English was Japanese.

She focused on the light and said, "*Denki o keshite kudasai.*" Please turn off the light.

This seemed to panic the light bulb. "I don't know if I should! This is very awkward!"

Jamie repeated her request more sternly. She heard a pop and the light went dark.

"Did I kill it?" Jamie asked, covering her mouth with one hand. "*Daijoubu desu ka?*" Are you okay?

"I... hurt..." the light bulb said, its voice faint.

Cole gingerly unscrewed the light bulb and shook it near his ear. "You burnt it out."

Jamie felt ill at what she had done. "I just talked a light bulb spirit into committing suicide."

"Light bulbs burn out all the time."

"And people die all the time, but I don't go around murdering people."

"Okay, well... I guess we should focus on some other exercises then."

~

Jamie sat in Shambalah Coffeehouse, nursing her coffee and wishing her headache would go away. Pain relief medicine hadn't taken a dent out of it.

By the time she had left Bifrost, she had convinced skates to skate on their own, chairs to swivel, and lamps to turn off without having the light bulbs commit suicide. She also left with a pounding headache. She woke up with a pounding headache. And spent the whole day with a headache.

"Dave?" she asked, her voice thin and strained. "Do you have any good cures for headaches?"

Dave paused in bussing the table nearby and thought about the question. "The Dalai Lama once said, 'Buddha's full teachings dispel the pain of worldly existence and self-oriented peace.'"

"Since when are you a Buddhist?" Jamie asked.

"Since I was a young boy," Dave said.

"I didn't know that."

Dave shrugged. "You never asked. But I didn't choose 'Shambalah' at random."

"So how is the Dalai Lama supposed to help with a headache?"

He smiled. "This is where I hold up a flower and you obtain enlightenment."

Jamie rested her head on the table and whimpered. She'd rather be home, but Ashley convinced her to come. Parker had avoided Jamie all morning. Not knowing what else to do, Jamie had gone to Ashley for advice, and Ashley offered to mediate any conversation. So there Jamie sat, waiting for Parker and Ashley to come and hash things out.

A few minutes later, something cold rattled next to Jamie's head. She looked up to see a plastic bag filled with ice next to her. She rested her head on that and groaned, "Thank you, Dave."

She lifted her head when she heard the door open and saw Parker and Ashley come in. Dave frowned as they walked through, and Ashley returned his look questioningly, but neither said anything. Ashley sat down next to Jamie while Parker remained standing.

Jamie rubbed away the damp spot on her forehead from the ice pack and smiled. "Hey you."

Parker just glared back.

"You look awful, Jamie," Ashley said, eyes wide with concern.

"I've had the worst headache all day."

"Out living it up with your new best friend?" Parker asked.

"Yes," Jamie said. "Non-stop thrills. The roof was both raised and on fire."

Parker rolled her eyes.

"Look, I'm sorry that I can't tell you right now. Give me some time and this may change, but this is something I need to work through."

"Work through how?" Parker yelled. "Hanging out with a fat old guy at a roller rink?"

Jamie winced, Parker's volume driving through her head like a nail. Jamie could not have imagined Parker being this angry.

"You know what?" Parker said. "Screw this. I don't know why I even bothered to come here. I'm just sorry I wasted money on a Homecoming dress."

As Parker walked away, a chill of dread ran through Jamie. "Parker?"

The other girl stopped but didn't turn back.

"Will you check your bag for an apple?" Jamie asked.

"Why the hell would I have an apple?"

"Just humor me."

Parker dug through her bag and pulled out an apple with a word carved into it. She frowned in confusion and threw it towards Jamie, who caught it without even thinking about it. Parker resumed heading towards the exit.

"Good luck keeping the doctor away," Parker said before walking out the door.

Jamie rested her head on her icepack again. She wondered how serious Parker was about vengeance running in her family.

"I guess it's just as well," Ashley said. "I don't know what has her so mad, but if she can't respect your privacy, then maybe you don't want her around."

Jamie felt someone pull the apple from her hand and looked over to see Dave sitting on the other side of her. He looked at the apple and then set it down next to him.

"You seem biased," he said.

"I've had a lot of people turn on me," Ashley said, her tone reserved. She kept darting looks at the apple. "If they don't value me, then why should I value them?"

"Stubborn pride is a difficult weight to bear."

"Pride is what keeps your head above water when the world is against you."

Dave shook his head. "Pride is more what keeps others away from you who might help you. Or keep you from helping those who might need it."

"It's a dog-eat-dog world."

"Only if you look at it that way," Dave suggested.

"Do you have a better way?" Ashley asked.

Jamie looked up at the two of them. Ashley looked tense, glaring at Dave. Dave just looked sad and tired. Dave usually kept his interactions with people light and casual, so she didn't understand why he had decided to tangle with Ashley.

"People are just people. Hurt, flawed, grasping. They're shaped by the world around them. And they shape others in a blind, stumbling fashion. To assume that each person who hurts you is out to get you is like assuming that the wind is plotting against you. They are no more or less deserving of kindness, regardless of their flaws, than you are."

Ashley snorted derisively. "Did that get you through high

school?"

"I never went to high school. But I do know that there are stars that have been dead for thousands of years by the time their light reaches Earth. When facing such cosmic scope, how can you think that some snub is that important?"

"If our feelings, our passions, aren't important, what's the use in living?" Ashley asked.

Dave shrugged. "In time, you will die, so every moment is worth savoring. Your passions, your anger... they get in the way of that. If you prefer to be miserable, you are welcome to continue clinging on to your attachments. If you want to be happy, though, you may want to consider a different approach."

Ashley turned her attention towards Jamie, pointedly ignoring Dave. "Are you going to be okay?"

"My head hurts so bad, I can't find it in me to be upset. I'll probably feel miserable once I feel better." She pushed herself slowly out of her chair and began to shuffle her way towards the door. "I'm going to go home and try to get some sleep. Maybe that will help my head enough so that I'll be ready to beat it against another wall."

~

Jamie glared at the large, black Viking in roller skates, the spirit of Bifrost Roller Rink, that stood in front of her as she stretched her hand towards him and said, "*Koko ni kinasai.*" Come here.

He looked at her with amusement and confusion. "I'm standing right here, girl. I'm not getting any closer."

She paused in her effort to cock her head in annoyance. "Will you please just stop with the commentary? *Kuru!*"

Her nap had helped her headache significantly, but tonight's exercises were not helping. Since she'd been successful in getting spirits to make changes to the physical world, she was now trying to physically contact a spirit while Cole repaired skates in the back room of Bifrost.

She repeated the phrase over and over again, chanting it like the *nembutsu*. Pain built up in her head, but she refused to give up before she did this. Her vision swam from the pain and she felt herself swaying. She stumbled forward, tears running down her face, and strong hands caught her and kept her from falling.

"Thank you," she muttered, resting her head against the leather on the other person's chest.

Leather?

She bolted upright and looked at the equally surprised face of Bifrost's spirit. She staggered back and began to fall. The spirit tried to catch her again but she passed through his hands and collided with the table. She heard running and soon saw Cole standing above her.

"You alright?"

"I did it. I touched a spirit. But now I think I broke something."

"A rib?" Cole asked.

She shook her head. "I think my brain."

Cole reached down and slowly helped her up. "Okay, let's get some water into you and see if that helps."

Jamie let herself be led back to one of the benches and sipped slowly at the ice water that Cole handed her. The cold felt better, and her headache slowly began to fade.

"Did all of your shamans get splitting headaches from their powers?" she asked.

"I never saw them get any, but they may have gotten good enough that they didn't get them anymore. I imagine your power is like a muscle, and the more you exercise it, the stronger it gets."

"So you're saying you've pushed me too hard?"

"If you aren't able to take on Eris, then I'll know I didn't push you hard enough."

Someone banged on the glass doors at the front of the skating rink. Cole leaned over to look towards the entrance, then shrugged. "Just some skels, probably freezing their asses off and looking for some place warm to hole up in."

"You are in trouble," the spirit of Bifrost said. "This place is under attack."

Jamie turned to look at the spirit. "We're under attack?"

Cole looked at her in surprise. "What do you mean we're under attack?"

"That's just what the rink spirit said."

The sound of shattering glass drew their attention back towards the front. The homeless people Cole had mentioned walked into view, bundled in mismatched clothing. An owl flew past them and changed into human form as it landed. It looked like another homeless person.

Cole stood up and began backing away from the intruders. "I'm guessing these are your *strixes*?"

"Looks like."

"I never figured Eris to be the sort to reach out towards the downtrodden."

Jamie moved back with him, hands raised in a defensive posture. "No, it fits. The students she recruited from the school are all the misfits and outcasts. The uninvited. This fits with the general theme."

"Well, great," Cole said. "I'd hate to think that the goddess was just being inconsistent. It's really great that she's empowering the disenfranchised."

"I'll remember to tell her that as I punch her face in."

One of the *strixes* charged Jamie. She side-stepped it and used its momentum to throw it through a table.

"Do we have a plan?" Jamie asked. The *strix* she threw dusted himself off and seemed unharmed.

"I'm making my way back to the emergency exit." He gestured towards the red-painted doors, and they heard banging and saw it rattle.

"I think someone anticipated that," Jamie said.

A *strix* launched himself at Cole and knocked him down. Jamie kicked the attacker in the face while he tried to bite Cole, but soon found two more *strixes* jumping on her. She struggled in their superhuman grips but couldn't seem to get loose. As she felt them dragging her down to the ground she screamed out, "Bifrost-*sama*, *tasukete kudasai*!" Bifrost, help me!

One of the homeless men stumbled and fell, allowing Jamie to break free of the grip of the other one and get away. Behind the *strix* that held her captive, she saw the spirit of the roller rink holding on to a smaller, struggling spirit that looked like an owl. Both Bifrost and the owl looked surprised by the situation.

Cole had escaped from his attacker and pulled back into the office. Jamie ran through the door and they shut themselves in, bolted the door and wedged a chair under the knob just in case. More *strixes* banged on the door while Cole stumbled into a seat and clutched a hand to his chest.

Jamie saw this and felt panic course through her. "You are *not* having a heart attack."

"Remember that when my daughter asks about tonight. Assure

her that everything was fine and I didn't have any sort of heart problems."

"You're having a heart attack?" Jamie leaned against the wall. She could not deal with both a heart attack and an army of *strixes*.

"No… I think it's just angina. I hope it's just angina."

"How will you know?" Jamie heard her voice squeak.

"Well, when we see the Valkyries come to take me to Valhalla, we'll know it was probably a heart attack. But I'm pretty sure it's just angina."

"I don't know what angina is, but I'm going to assume that it means that your heart is filled with ponies and rainbows and it's a positive thing."

"You're one of those, aren't you?"

"One of whats?"

"The more scared you get, the more of a smartass you become."

"Screw you. We need to get you out of here. Do you have any weapons?"

"I keep a baseball bat in case I'm here when vandals show up, but that's about it."

"I can't take a mob of vampire owls with a baseball bat! I had trouble with three when I had a katana!"

"Well, I'm not a religious man, so I don't have crosses or anything."

"You were a Norse god and you didn't become religious?"

"You don't want to worship gods after having been one!"

"I've got my *onenju* in my bag, but that's more of a one-on-one tool."

"What the hell's an *onenju*?"

The sound of splintering wood drew her attention towards the door. "Poopsticks. Okay, what can I work with here?"

She scanned the small cluttered office. Forms, receipts, pencils, pens, cellophane tape, a dust-caked computer monitor, roller skates… This was an awful place to make a last stand. She wished she knew how to make a bigger holy symbol. Her *onenju* was probably mass produced in China or something, but it did the job of stopping *strixes*.

Then she stopped and had an idea. She grabbed one of the receipts and a pen and, after making sure the pen worked, she began writing out the *nembutsu* on the scrap of paper. When she'd filled the paper she grabbed a loose skate wheel and taped the paper onto it.

"What the hell are you doing?" Cole asked.

"In Tibetan Buddhism, they have prayer wheels in front of some temples. They have the mantra of infinite compassion on them, and by spinning the wheel you send the mantra out into the world." She stuck the wheel on top of the pen and spun it. It wobbled on its bearings. "I don't know the mantra, but I do know the *nembutsu*, which is about the holiest thing I believe in. So either this will be a wicked area effect holy symbol, or we're *strix* chow."

She took her impromptu prayer wheel to the door and spun it. The banging on the door stopped. She smiled hopefully and opened the door before giving the wheel another spin. As the door swung slowly open, she could see the homeless people pulling away from the office and cowering in fear. She kept spinning it and Cole slowly shuffled behind her. She glanced back, saw that he had an ashy gray complexion and assumed that was bad.

They made it to Cole's car in the parking lot, an old looking Dodge Charger. Cole handed Jamie his keys. Jamie looked at them in panic. "What am I supposed to do with these?"

"I'm in no state to drive," Cole said as he went around the car to the passenger side, leaning heavily on the car as he went.

"I don't have a license!"

"Well, consider this a driving lesson from Uncle Cole," he gasped.

The *strixes* began pushing forward again and Jamie spun the wheel to push them back. She got into the driver's seat and fumbled to get the keys into the ignition as the *strixes* came along side and began banging and rocking the car. The engine started and she gunned it forward. A block later, she remembered to put on her seat belt. Jamie felt sick with fear. She'd driven a car some for practice, but she didn't have a lot of experience. And none of that prepared her for a high speed chase with owls.

Behind her, owls flew on silent downy wings. Pedestrians pointed at them in surprise but were not that thrown off. This was Cobalt City, after all.

"Do you know where the nearest hospital is?" Jamie asked. She didn't know West Key at all.

Cole shook his head. "No hospitals."

"But you're having an angina attack, whatever that is." She

slammed on the brakes to avoid T-boning another driver in the intersection. The car fishtailed and a few owls collided with the back of the car. When the intersection was clear Jamie gunned it again. "You need, like, a doctor."

"No. We go to a hospital, they start asking questions. Police get involved. Your secret identity is compromised, mine is… other people's. We need to keep this on the down low."

"I know a doctor who can help… but she's up in Morriston. And we have vampire owls chasing us."

"Do you have anyone else who can help?" Cole asked.

"No. Stardust called me, but his phone number didn't register in my phone. Do you still have the phone he sent you?"

"Hell no. It self-destructed."

"I don't have contact info for Huntsman or Libertine. I think Malenfant would really kill me if I dragged more bad guys to his house. Oh, wait. Idea."

"Great?"

Jamie pressed the gas pedal as hard as she could and headed north into Karlsburg, scraping alongside another car as she went. Sparks flew between them until the other car veered off to the side and crashed into a tree. She was certain if this kept up, she was going to get someone killed and probably herself. She slowed a little and focused on the car itself. *"Kuruma-sama tetsudatte kudasai!"* Spirit of the car, please help me!

"What sort of help you need, sweet thing?" the spirit asked from the backseat in a deep baritone. He reminded Jamie of Grandma Brown's R&B records from the 70s.

Jamie cranked the wheel to the right, and the car slid sideways several feet, before it moved forward again and onto the bridge over the Puckwudgie River. "I need help driving or we're going to die. Help keep this car safe."

"Darlin', I can tell you how to take care of this car but I'm just a ghost in this world."

"That wasn't a request." She mentally reached back and pulled the spirit towards her while screaming, *"Tasukete!"*

Her control over the car seemed easier but her head throbbed again. Now she just had to worry about the owls that were somehow keeping pace behind her.

Once over the bridge, they entered the winding streets of Karlsburg. She had to go slower here, but still pushed it as hard as she thought she could. She cut across lawns, outdoor café seating, and clipped a few building corners as she raced through the neighborhood. Soon she saw the roof of the church, its wisteria logo visible from the street lights. She didn't bother to look for parking, but drove onto the sidewalk and slammed on the brakes in front of the steps.

Agyo stood in front of the door, his *vajra* club in one hand as he looked at the owls raining down on the church. "Jamie? You are totally my best friend forever. Ungyo is out of luck."

And then the spirit leapt towards the owls, cleaving through the first one he encountered. His club crushed the spirit form of an owl while the physical body changed back into human form and crashed into the steps. He did not pause, but continued swinging his weapon in a deadly arc. Spiritual blood and feathers sprayed through the air and the former hosts fell unconscious as mortals once again.

Jamie ducked low in her seat while the few *strixes* that broke through Agyo's assault pounded on the car in an attempt to break it open. Before they could cause any serious damage, they collapsed as Agyo destroyed the possessing spirits. Soon the few *strixes* who escaped the guardian spirit's club flew off into the night.

Agyo lowered his face to the driver's side window. "That was the coolest thing ever. They were like piñatas filled with greed, hatred and delusion."

"If I could hug you, Agyo, I would. Thank you so much for saving us."

"No sweat, kiddo. This was the most fun I've had in years." He walked towards the street and yelled, "Hear that, Methodist angel? How do you like that? How many demons you get to smack down, huh?"

Jamie asked, "Spirit of the car?"

The spirit sounded weak. "Yeah?"

"I need your help pulling out of here without running over any unconscious bums or running into a car."

"That better be all you want, girl. I'm about worn out from your last favor."

~

The storm arose out of nowhere and descended upon Dr.

Hao's house with a fury. Looking out the front windows, Jamie could believe it was the end of the world. She felt more certain of it when Cleopatra, or Tera, if she wanted to use her real name, drove her car up onto the doctor's lawn and left it running as she got out.

Jamie went over to the door to let Cole's daughter in, but it exploded inward and flew off its hinges trailing smoke and flames. Tera walked into the living room and looked at Jamie with fury in her eyes. Lightning bolts ran up and down the woman's arms and sparked around her eyes.

Doctor Hao called out, "You had best power down before you make your father's problem worse."

Jamie looked over to see the doctor dressed in rubber boots and gloves with a rubber apron, holding a fire extinguisher. Apparently, she prepared for anything. Tera's electrical manifestations died down but did not entirely go away. She turned her attention towards Jamie.

"I want you to get the hell away from my father," she said. Jamie started to protest but the lightning surged around Tera. "This isn't an option. I'm not stupid. I can feel the power coming off of you. I know you've been to the rink. I'm guessing he's been teaching you how to be a hero. The man can't even hide his secret stash of doughnuts. Hiding his secret training missions? I let it go for a bit, but that's just got to stop. He nearly died once. He's too old and unhealthy to be teaching any newbie masks, let alone one bringing Lord knows what down on his head. So I want you to turn your ass around and get the hell out of this place before I make you leave this place. If I get any word that Dad is training you again, you will know what the wrath of a God means. Do I make myself clear?"

Jamie nodded and waited for Tera to continue on into the house, leaving scorch marks with each step, before walking out the front door. She wondered if her dad could give her a ride home.

CHAPTER 17 - AWKWARD CONVERSATIONS

Jamie sat in the lunch room, staring at her enchiladas. She poked at one with her spork, but couldn't find the will to eat it. She heard a plastic tray set on her table. From the edge of her vision, she saw a short pleated skirt.

"Go away, Sabrina."

"I'm surprised. I thought your first question would be why I'm here."

"I'm sure it makes sense in crazy cheerleader logic and would only make me feel more dumb."

"Justin's worried about you."

"He better worry for himself if he puts his tray on this table again," Jamie growled.

"What? Are you going to break his other arm?"

Jamie looked up at Sabrina.

Sabrina sat there with her food uneaten. "Where are your loser friends?"

Jamie looked back down at her food. "Is it any of your business?"

"Actually, it was a rhetorical question. I know Parker is avoiding you. But Ashley missing is odd. Is she going to appear on our wall of missing losers?"

Jamie closed her eyes and took a long breath, mentally chanting the *nembutsu*. Tears threatened at the edge of her eyes, but she wouldn't give Sabrina the satisfaction of seeing her break. Jamie wasn't sure how she felt about dating a girl, but she knew she didn't like losing Parker like this. She sat up straight and looked over at Sabrina again. "Would you be happy if she was?"

"Well, if she can't get her crap together, she may as well not be here."

"What crap does she need to get together?"

"Losers like Ashley just love wallowing in their self-pity. They need to put on their big girl panties and make something of themselves."

"So it's their fault that you and every other bully at this school kick them down on a regular basis?"

Sabrina pulled her head back in surprise. "I am not a bully."

"Then what do you call your constant demeaning attitude?"

"I work hard. My family isn't well off like Ashley's. I scrimp and save and fight tooth and claw to get everything I have. She shows up, fat, ugly, awkward, and rich, then she expects us to feel bad for her and give her a break. If they can't keep up with a head start, they aren't worth my respect."

"So because Ashley's probably been picked on by other kids all her life and suffers because of it, she's not worth treating like a person?"

"I don't cut anyone slack. Everyone I associate with either earns their place with me or is useful."

"Really?" Jamie asked. She pitched her voice higher, "Like, ohmygod Brina, really?" Sabrina glared in response to the funny voice so Jamie switched back. "Then why the hell do you keep bothering me? Don't you have other people worth your time? I can't imagine why I'd be useful to you."

Sabrina used that opportunity to take a bite of food.

"Is this all because of Parker?" Jamie asked. "Are you worried I'll get sent to a camp? Or are you trying to validate your own brainwashing by trying to break my will too?"

Sabrina opened her mouth and took a deep breath, blinking rapidly. In a hoarse voice she asked, "She told you that?"

"Ashley did. I guess the rumors spread at camp afterwards."

Sabrina stood up with her tray. "Well, this was clearly a mistake. I won't waste my time with you anymore."

Jamie watched as the cheer captain dumped the contents of her still-full tray into the trash and left the cafeteria.

~

The motel sat in the southeastern part of Karlsburg, near the edge of the Hollows. In the dim streetlights, with the icy wind off the Puckwudgie River winding through the streets, it seemed even worse. It wasn't the worst part of town, but it definitely lived next door to it. Jamie couldn't understand why her mother would be all the way out here, but it was the address Grandma Brown had given her.

The address also came with the instruction, "You tell that fool mother of yours that she needs to get her head out of her ass and get back home."

The room was at ground level with an outside entry, the blue paint on the door chipped and faded. Jamie recognized her mom's car in front of the motel room. The front passenger side window had been broken and clear plastic had been taped up in its place.

Jamie walked up to the door and knocked. She heard footsteps approach the door, and a long pause before the door opened.

"Did you bus here?" Gloria asked. Jamie expected rage on her mother's face, but her mother just looked tired and sad.

"Yes."

"This isn't a safe part of town."

"I'm not worried about my safety. Why are you way out here?"

Her mother shrugged. "It was inexpensive enough for me to stay a while before deciding what to do next."

"And what are you thinking of doing?"

Gloria ignored the last question. "What do you want, Jamie?"

"I want you to come home."

"Your father and I had an understanding. He broke that understanding."

"No, I broke that understanding without knowing about it."

"He admitted that he knew about it."

"What was he supposed to do?" Jamie asked. "He couldn't stop me without telling me about your agreement."

"He could have told me."

"So you could have left earlier?"

"That isn't fair."

"I don't think you've been fair for years," Jamie said.

"This coming from someone who knew how I felt about vigilantes but went out with a mask and three feet of sharpened steel to stop crime on her own?"

"I had to."

"You're seventeen. What you had to do was finish school. If you needed to clean up the streets, you could join a neighborhood watch until you were old enough to enter the police academy."

"Do you think I liked it?" Jamie yelled. "Do you think I enjoyed lying to you? If I could not do it I would, but… but…" She lost steam. She felt weird telling her mother that she could see spirits and see them in pain, and shut her mouth before she said anything more. She felt off balance and out of her element.

Gloria frowned. "You see things, don't you?"

Jamie's eyes widened in surprise. She didn't know what to say.

"Grandma Brown will be pleased when she finds out."

"W-what? Why?"

Gloria looked out towards the street, away from Jamie. "Because she was disappointed I wasn't able to see them."

"Shut up. Grandma Brown was not a superhero." Jamie had seen pictures of her grandma from when she was young in the 70s. She could not imagine that the woman with bellbottoms and a monster afro had worn tights and fought crime.

"No, she wasn't. But she believed that angels helped her solve crimes. She worked as a consultant for the police for a few years until she got married and decided to raise a family."

"Why didn't anyone tell me before?"

"I don't know why she did anything she did, but Mom didn't like to tell people about her ability. I imagine she thought she was being 'humble before the Lord' or something. If He gave her an ability, it wasn't proper to brag about it. As for me… I never told your father. At first because it wasn't for me to tell. Then, later, because he'd use it against me. But Mom said this would happen. That you would see these things and want to act. You're not a young sleuth. We raised you to beat people up, so I guess that's the tool you're going to use."

They stood in silence on the doorstep to the motel room for several minutes. Jamie broke the silence first.

"Will you come home?"

"I can't. Your father lied to me for too long."

"He only knew for a few weeks," Jamie pointed out. "And he may have been trying to decide what to say to you."

Gloria hesitated, then shook her head.

"I need you there, Mom. Dad gets weird that I've been seeing Parker. Or was until 2thefairest slipped Parker an apple whammy." When Jamie saw her mom's confused expression she said, "Sorry, I've had a Greek god ruining my life. But that's not the point. The point is, I don't think he's comfortable with it. I've never had a relationship and I don't know anything about dating a girl and I don't know if I'll find someone else and I need to know that you'll have my back."

Her mom pulled Jamie into a hug. "Let me think about it. I may have to have your back from another house, but you're still my little girl. I can't support you wearing a mask, but I will help you with your love life if you want it."

Jamie sobbed. "Thank you, Mom."

CHAPTER 18 - TO CATCH A GOD

Kensei stood on the roof of Lincoln High, looking at the shrine she had built for Abe. She needed to get some answers and had a way to get them. Cole had said that having a focus helped. With her costume on and her sword at her side, she couldn't get more in character if she tried.

She gripped the hilt of her katana, focused on bringing the spirit to her, and called out, "Abe, *koko ni kinasai.*"

Abe looked surprised as he jolted into view in front of her. He looked even more surprised when she grabbed him by the front of his flannel shirt and dragged him closer. His clothing felt ephemeral, and she felt like someone was trying to slowly push a broom handle through her forehead, but Abe didn't have to know that.

"You backed the wrong horse, Abe. And now you have some explaining to do."

"W-what do you want?"

"I need to know who 2thefairest is, or I will beat you to a bloody pulp."

"But the school... If you hurt me—"

"If the goddess of strife keeps things up, she's going to tear this school apart anyway. You can either help me stop her, or we can see how long I can beat on you before something breaks."

"I am bound by oaths not to give her name," Abe said. Kensei shook him by the shirt. He felt like he might slip out of her grasp, but instead he yelped before adding, "But I can point you towards her. Please, come downstairs into the school."

Abe led Kensei across the roof to a skylight and helped her to bypass the security alarm before she dropped down into the halls of the school. Some of the lights were still on, leaving Kensei feeling vulnerable. He led her down towards the area of her locker and pointed at a locker across from her own. She couldn't remember whose locker number this was.

"What's the combination?" she asked.

"This is as far as I go. You want the locker opened, you can open it."

Kensei focused on the locker door. "*Doa o akete kudasai.*" Open the door.

Another bolt of pain shot through Kensei's skull as the locker opened. The inside was unadorned. Just books, school supplies and a black cloth bag. From the shape of it she could tell what it was before she opened it: apples. She pulled out one of the notebooks and flipped through it until she found a name: Ashley Jones.

She rested her head against the edge of the locker, not sure what she was going to do about this. Could she fight Ashley? And an army of *strixes*?

The squeak of a tennis shoe on linoleum broke her out of her reverie. She looked up to see Sabrina standing in the hall. Kensei drew her sword, hoping that the blade would keep Sabrina away long enough to escape.

Sabrina rolled her eyes. "Really, Jamie? Am I supposed to believe you'd stab me?"

Kensei froze, blood pounding in her ears.

"Can you put away your sword and take off that stupid mask so we can talk?" When Kensei didn't respond, Sabrina said, "Look, I've known who you are since I saw you on my lawn. If I was going to tell anyone, I would have done it a long time ago. If you were looking into the blog, I figured that this must be part of you wearing a stupid mask so I asked Justin to help you."

Kensei sheathed the sword but left her mask on. "What do you want?"

Sabrina looked over into the locker and poked at the bag with all the apples. "Whose locker is this?"

"Ashley's."

"Why are you going through Ashley's locker?"

"Because she's behind the blog."

"Let me guess, this is about more than just a blog?"

"How did you find me here?" Jamie asked, ignoring the question.

"There was a football game tonight. I was on the way back to my car when I noticed someone sneaking around on the roof. Figured it was you. What's so special about Ashley and her blog?"

"I think Ashley is the avatar of Eris, goddess of strife."

Sabrina's eyes widened in alarm. "Are you serious? She has some sort of superpower and she's evil? This is why I keep trying to get my parents to move to Boston."

"Evil's a strong word…"

"And you're friends with her?" Sabrina shook her head, her swinging ponytail echoing her disdain.

"I… I didn't know it was her. I thought she was helping me… but I think she was just feeding me false leads."

"We need to call the cops."

Kensei shook her head. "If we call the cops, she goes to jail. I want to give her a chance to back down before I ruin her life more."

"But… but she…" Sabrina clenched her fists in frustration. "Fine. Fine. Whatever. Fine. Go do whatever the hell you have to do. Just leave me out of it."

Kensei couldn't believe that Sabrina didn't put up more of an argument. The cheerleader had turned and walked away before Kensei realized something embarrassing. "Um, Sabrina. I don't have a car. Can you give me a ride to Ashley's?"

"Fine," Sabrina said without turning back. "But you have to take off that retarded mask before you get in my car."

~

The ride out to Ashley's neighborhood was awkward. Sabrina focused on the road and ignored Jamie. The spirit of Sabrina's car, a guy named Cristobal who held a staff and carried a child on his shoulder, insisted the whole time that Jamie get her heathen beliefs away from Sabrina before she spread them. Since the spirit was shaped by his driver, she wondered what this said about Sabrina.

Once over at Ashley's neighborhood, Jamie had Sabrina park her car a block away. Slipping her mask back on, Kensei skulked through backyards, staying at the edges to avoid motion sensor lights as she headed towards the Jones residence. She tried to keep track of any police calls on her scanner that would indicate that she'd been spotted.

The backyard to Ashley's house lacked the polish of the front, but still looked well kept. A deck extended from the back door full of a BBQ grill and patio furniture. She slipped across the deck and winced as the back porch light came on. She crouched low and looked around for any sign she had been noticed.

Kensei turned to the wooden door, which had a window covering the top half, and said, "Open" in Japanese. The door did not respond at all. Not even to tell her, "No."

She struck the glass with the pommel of her sword, then reached through and unlocked it.

The door opened into the kitchen, which smelled of dust and the sickly sweet odor of rotting food. The trash and counters were filled with empty pizza boxes and fast food packages. Kensei tried to identify any spirits nearby, but they all felt distant. She guessed that made sense. If you were going to mess with someone who could talk to spirits, you'd make sure that none would blab on you. That included Karl and probably even Glenda. Ashley probably bullied the school spirit because it would be more inclined to bend to her will. Or maybe it would be too obvious if the spirit just disappeared.

The kitchen led into the dining room, then connected with the living room. Sitting in the living room were an older man and woman, probably in their 30s or 40s. A thick layer of dust coated them. Kensei stepped over to touch one and check for a pulse. Though their bodies felt icy cold, she could feel a faint pulse. She wondered how long they had sat there like that.

The only remaining doors on the first floor led to a half bath and the garage, so Kensei went up the stairs. Ashley's room was obvious, with a poster of a unicorn and light spilling out from under the door. Kensei crept close and listened, but could hear nothing. She took a few steps back, then ran at the door, breaking through the thin plywood.

Kensei stumbled a bit and looked around. The room was a mess, with piles of laundry lying everywhere. In the center of the room was a table with a Starcom tablet propped up on top. It flickered to life and Ashley's face appeared there, somber and serious.

"Hi, Jamie. Or is it appropriate to call you Kensei? I'm never sure of the etiquette."

"The mask is on, so Kensei."

"Right. Well, I'm really sorry about this. You've been a great friend and all I did was lie to you."

"Where are you? What's going on with your parents?"

"Well, I'll get to where in a moment. But I wanted to share a fun fact: Did you know that some people believe that *Sleeping Beauty* is derived from the myth of Eris? Only instead of a goddess at a wedding it's a fairy at a christening. It wasn't easy, but because enough people believe that Eris is the fairy from *Sleeping Beauty*, I was able to create the same effect. I don't get to brag very often about this, so I have to take every opportunity to explain."

"I'm surprised you didn't put the whole school to sleep."

"If people are asleep, it's harder to make them miserable. And this is about bringing strife."

"So, where are you?" Kensei said casually.

"Well, first let me tell you that I had the school watched. I did what I could to button down the spirit there without making my actions overly obvious. But just in case, I warded things so that I'd know if he blabbed. He was the weak link in my cover and he cracked in the end. So, now I've had to take out insurance." The view in the screen shot up to the ceiling and then shifted around a bit as Ashley changed the angle of her camera to point behind her. Hanging by bound hands, Parker twisted in an attempt to break the bonds. Duct tape covered her mouth.

The police scanner in Kensei's ear crackled to life. "All units, we have a burglary in progress at 2323 Yossarian Avenue. Please respond."

Then, "Dispatch this is Car 27, responding."

The camera pointed back to Ashley. "I'm in the old warehouse for Cobalt City Frozen Foods, down by the river. It's a little hard to find on GPS, so I left you a little map on the back of the Starpad. Please come. It'll be fun."

The tablet shut off. Kensei grabbed it, tore the map off the back of the tablet and tossed the Starpad aside. Running out at ground level seemed like it would end like a bad episode of *Cops*. She slid open Ashley's window and reached out to grab the rain gutter and pull herself up. It groaned under her weight but she made it to the roof without plummeting to her death.

She gauged distances to nearby houses and aimed for the closest one with a running leap. She slid on the steep slope, kicking loose shingles in the process but hurrying to get her feet under her and jump over to the next one until she was clear of the area. She wondered what the police would think when they found Mr. and Mrs. Jones asleep in the house.

At the last house on the block, she climbed down towards the back, keeping the house between her and the street. She saw Sabrina driving by in her station wagon, so she ran for the passenger side door. Sabrina pulled to a stop long enough to allow Kensei to climb in.

"I thought you were going to wait for me," Jamie said as she pulled off her mask.

"I was, and then a cop came and told me I couldn't just loiter there. So I've been trying to drive around randomly and circle back to where I was. Get over yourself. Did you murder Ashley or whatever it is you do with your frog poker?"

"No. She's not there. Instead, she had a Starpad there and was broadcasting live from her supervillain lair where she has Parker captive."

Sabrina rolled her eyes. "How cliché. I hope you're not expecting me to charge a supervillain lair with you."

"No, but I would like a ride down to the river if you can manage it. Then I need you to get help."

"The police?"

"No, actually—"

Sabrina rolled her eyes. "Leave it to you to avoid the common sense approach."

"I'm trying to help Ashley."

"The same person who kidnapped your dyke ex-girlfriend?"

"Look, will you just find some way to get hold of Stardust and emphasize that this is an emergency?"

Sabrina snorted in amusement. "Oh, sure, like Stardust will take my call."

"I'm sure you'll come up with something."

~

Jamie spent the car ride with her head against the cold glass of the passenger side window. Her head ached from pushing her power. Nausea lingered at the edge of her awareness as she watched the neighborhood turn from houses to warehouses and factories. Sabrina didn't talk, which didn't bother Jamie too much. She was too busy trying to get rid of her headache before she pushed her power again.

Still, Jamie couldn't believe how upside down everything had become. Ashley was a villain, Sabrina was a friend. Combined with her headache and the cold darkness outside of the car, it made her feel like she had entered some new bizarre world where nothing made sense.

She turned and looked at Sabrina. The cheerleader was only visible in silhouette against the infrequent street lights passing outside. As if feeling Jamie's gaze, she glanced over for a second before turning her attention back to the road.

"Staring at me again?" Sabrina asked.

"Why are you doing this? Why are you going through all this effort to help me?"

"I have a soft spot for charity cases."

Jamie started to laugh, but it spiked the pain in her head and she stopped. "No, you don't. You hate charity cases. I can't think of anything you would like about me."

"Then I don't have an answer for you."

Jamie frowned as she tried to think around the pain in her head. It couldn't be about Parker. Sabrina had been helping her before Parker was in trouble. In retrospect, most of the help she'd received had nothing to do with Jamie dating Parker.

Was Sabrina connected with the cape and cowl scene somehow, like Dr. Hao? Was Jamie just useful to Sabrina's plans? Could Sabrina be a supervillain in training? Jamie just didn't know. She glanced back at the spirit in the back seat, wondering if he had any answers. But he only glared at Jamie.

Sabrina stopped the car and pulled the emergency brake, leaving the car idling. "We're here."

Jamie looked over at the chain link fence with the barbed wire along the top. Every twenty feet, a sign said, "NO TRESPASSING" in big red letters.

"Sure I can't talk you out of this?" Sabrina asked. "I understand the police are pretty used to dealing with superpowered threats, more so than ever before."

"No, I want to try and get Ashley out of this. I don't want to destroy her life by getting her locked up at the Fermi Institute like every other mentally disturbed supervillain."

Sabrina nodded, her gaze locked forward. She didn't say anything else.

"Well," Jamie said. "Guess I should go." She turned and pulled the handle on the door, causing the dome light in the car to turn on.

"Wait," Sabrina said.

Jamie looked back. Sabrina had turned to look at her, frowning. Then, without warning, she leaned over and awkwardly hugged Jamie.

At first, Jamie tensed up, half expecting an attack. But the human contact was a surprising comfort. She relaxed and hugged Sabrina back. For a moment things seemed better, held in someone's arms. The smell of Sabrina was calming and pleasant.

Sabrina pulled back and went to looking forward again. "Be careful out there."

"I don't understand you," Jamie said.

Sabrina smirked. "I don't understand me either. If you tell anyone I hugged you, I'll reveal your secret identity to anyone who will listen."

Jamie opened her mouth in surprise, but decided she was too tired to deal with this. She turned and got out of the car.

CHAPTER 19 - GODS AND MONSTERS

Based on the map, the warehouse that Ashley had invited Kensei to was about a half mile from where Sabrina dropped her off. The surrounding area was industrial, with loading docks for boats sailing out to the Atlantic and factories positioned to dump their effluent out into the Puckwudgie. Spirits watched from the shadows: downtrodden, oppressed. The wind off the river was stronger here, carrying with it the chemical stench of pollution. Even with the smell, the dubiously fresh air made Jamie's head feet better.

Clutching her sword, Kensei focused on the spirit of the wind. Serpentine shapes flowed through the air around her, merging in and out of one another and eddying into tight coils as they spun.

"*Kaze-sama, tasukete kudasai!*" she yelled. Her words seemed to disappear as soon as she yelled them, swallowed by the wind. A cold ache crept into her bones.

The wind shifted and the smaller snakes around her merged into one that turned to look down upon her from above. Its scaly body extended out and down the river to the ocean. "And why should I, little girl?"

Kensei froze. This had never happened to her before. The possibility that she could bring something into the world that could kill her seemed very real as the translucent serpent lowered its head to get a closer look. She felt like she'd gone looking for fireworks and found a nuke.

"I require aid against the goddess Eris, who is waiting for me close to here."

"Until the goddess causes me trouble, I don't care where she lairs."

"She holds my girlfriend captive."

The serpent chuckled, causing the wind to coil about Kensei. "That sounds like your problem, not mine. I can tell you are trying to compel me. I would not bother. I am not some weak city spirit. I and my kind have prowled along the riverbed long before humans touched the ground here."

"Then what do you want?"

"Blood and prayer." When Kensei hesitated the spirit added. "Pig's blood will do. I understand you can obtain it at a butcher shop. Offer me a handful of your blood now, and give me a gallon of pig's blood at this spot on the next new moon and I will aid you tonight. Fail me and you will know why the goblins of this city hid underground. What is it you wish of me?"

This deal was getting worse all the time. "I will be facing her *strixes*, more than I can probably deal with on my own. I need to be protected from them, perhaps keep them from flying at me." As she realized that the spirit might not play nice with others she added, "And please don't kill people."

"Then make it two gallons and we have a deal. Lead on."

Kensei hesitated. This sounded bad. She didn't know when she'd gone from simple magic tricks to deals with the devil. Tears pressed at her eyes. She could still walk away from this, but she didn't know that she could actually face an army of *strixes*, plus a goddess, on her own. Her plan had just been to make it harder for the *strixes* by having a wind spirit help keep them off. This was a whole level of awful that she couldn't get her mind around.

But then she thought of Parker tied up and gagged, and her decision was made. She drew her sword and peeled off one of her gloves. She cut her hand and watched the blood pool. Then she upturned her hand and spilled it out. Before it hit the ground, it faded from view and the serpent of air took on a hint of color. She mentally added another item to her "First Time" list. What had she conjured up? Could she put it down?

She looked at her hand and focused on the tiny spirits of flesh and blood that swarmed around it. She could see them already beginning to heal the wound. She mentally urged them to go faster and watched as the wound closed before her eyes. Her head threatened to explode from the effort.

She turned and jogged towards the warehouse. The pounding of blood in her temples caused her vision to dim from the pain. She clenched her jaw and ran through what few meditation techniques she knew. She focused on her breath, she mentally chanted the *nembutsu*. Anything to keep from falling over from the pain.

As she drew closer, she could see the owls watching her from the rooftops. Some just sat and watched, others took to the air but were buffeted by screaming winds and forced to land again. Further in, they came on foot. The winds pulled at them, lifting smaller *strixes* off their feet and slowing others. Kensei used the time to focus on her attackers as she tried to distinguish the possessing *strix* from the mortal host. She could barely make out wings looming behind them, even in human form. She rushed at the nearest one and sliced at the wings.

The man attacking her, one of the vagrants from Bifrost earlier, screamed in pain and collapsed. He looked like he was still breathing, but Kensei couldn't tell anything else before they attacked. She fought defensively, moving backwards in wide circles to keep them from swarming. When she saw openings, she sliced at more wings and watched them collapse.

As their numbers dwindled, fewer and fewer *strixes* dared engage her. She resumed running for the warehouse, the gravel of the driveway digging into her *tabi*. A *strix* sideswiped her despite the heavy winds and they both tumbled to the ground. Kensei felt hands clenched around her neck and looked up to see Courtney on top of her. Kensei flailed her wrist at Courtney and struck her with her *onenju*. Courtney recoiled away long enough for Kensei to regain her feet.

The two circled one another, Courtney staying just out of reach of the katana.

"You know," Kensei said, "When I offered to help you, I didn't mean that I'd lie down and die for you."

"It ends the same either way."

"Wow, what movie did you get that lame line from? Seriously, I'm going to get rid of the thing that's riding you. This can go easy or hard."

"I have power now," Courtney said. "I'm not giving that up."

"Hard it is." Kensei rushed towards Courtney, who turned into an owl and took flight, but flew out of control in the wind that raged about them. As Courtney flew overhead, Kensei grabbed one of the owl's legs and was dragged across the gravel driveway. She focused on the spirit form and swung at it as she made out the difference between the *strix* and Courtney. Kensei immediately found herself holding onto Courtney's ankle just as she fell on top of Kensei.

Kensei picked herself up off the ground and dusted off her costume. The door stood open, with a couple skinny kids from her school standing guard on either side. The inner circle, Kensei assumed. She ran at them, and barely slowed enough to cut their wings before continuing into the lair.

Owls perched all around the room, watching her from the rafters. The wind came in behind Kensei, roared upward, and scattered the birds. Some hit the ceiling and fell to the ground. The wind pushed others downward, hollow bones splintering against the concrete before they returned to more human forms. Before Kensei could act to bring her spirit to heel, an apple arced over the railing of the loft above her and bounced across the floor. The large serpent of wind became many smaller ones that turned upon each other. The winds evaporated, leaving only the sound of sobbing boys and girls lying in heaps on the floor. Kensei didn't want to think about the ramifications.

Kensei looked up to see Ashley at the railing, another apple in hand. She aimed it for Kensei, who cut through it with her sword. It fell to either side of her. Ashley threw more apples, which met a similar fate.

Kensei saw the stairs leading up and began staggering up them. More broken *strixes* lay on the steps, looking up at her through pain-clouded eyes. When she reached the loft, she saw Ashley waiting patiently with hands clasped demurely in front of her. Parker dangled off to the right, still and bound and gagged. Kensei fought off the urge to rush towards her girlfriend. Parker spotted Kensei and frowned in confusion.

"Jamie?" Parker seemed to say behind her duct tape gag. Or maybe, "Ninja." Heck, it could have been, "Bacon" for all Kensei could tell. It was really hard to understand sounds through duct tape.

"You've caught me," Ashley said.

"You made me a map. Ready to surrender?"

"I'm afraid I can't do that. You've been a good friend, Jamie.

But what I've found is that Eris won't give me a reprieve. You were part of my agreement with Eris: I could get my vengeance if she got to destroy your life. I thought I could resist her when I got to know you better. But she can be very persuasive. She won't let go of me. You're going to have to kill me."

"I'm not going to kill you," Kensei said.

Ashley shrugged. "Then send me to jail. Just know that Eris isn't going to give up on destroying you. Killing me is easier. I'm living on borrowed time anyway."

Kensei didn't ask for Ashley to elaborate, dreading what the answer might be. Instead she said, "I didn't come here to fight you. I came here to fight Eris."

"I'm afraid we're one and the same."

"I don't think so. Before I deal with Eris, I should probably get Parker free." She went over and sliced at the ropes that held Parker to the ceiling.

Parker dropped to her knees and rubbed at her wrists before reaching up and peeling off the duct tape. "I can't believe you. You gave me crap about wearing shorts over tights and you're a superhero?"

"Really?" Kensei asked as she knelt down beside Parker. She shook her head. "This is the first thing you want to say after I rescue you?"

Parker pouted. "I'm sorry I was a butthead when stupid Ashley slipped a magic apple into my backpack and made me psycho. I didn't know it was magic and then felt like such a butt afterwards that I couldn't face you."

Kensei reached out and pulled Parker into a hug, savoring the moment of rest. The whole world seemed wobbly now. Parker buried her face in Kensei's shoulder and sobbed.

"I'm sorry you got dragged into this," Kensei said. "And that I kept my secret identity a secret from you."

When Parker stopped crying, Kensei slowly disengaged from Parker and helped her stand. Kensei turned to Ashley and asked, "Do you have any weapons here?"

Ashley indicated boxes and crates against one side of the loft.

"C'mon Parker," Kensei said. "Let's pick something nice out for you."

"Why aren't we leaving?" Parker asked. "Ashley looks like she's done. Let's just boogie and go make out somewhere to celebrate."

"Because there's still one matter to deal with."

Kensei opened up what looked like a toybox with *Sesame Street* characters on it. Inside was a loose assortment of knives and clubs. Kensei picked out a nightstick and took it over to Parker, who was examining the contents of a crate. Inside was an unusual-looking gun nestled in packing material.

"Is that what I think it is?" Parker asked.

"A rocket propelled grenade launcher?" Kensei suggested.

"I was thinking a blasty doom gun, but if you want to be *technical...*"

Kensei offered the nightstick to Parker. "Here, I got you this."

"But doom gun...?"

"No."

Parker took the nightstick. "Damn you, voice of reason."

Kensei turned back to Ashley and drew her sword. "I know how to dispel the *strixes*. I may be able to use the same trick on Eris."

Ashley convulsed and clutched at her head. "No... no... I won't..."

Kensei focused on Ashley, trying to identify Eris the way she had with the *strixes* and figure out where the girl ended and the goddess began. She could see the struggle that Ashley put up to fight off Eris's control. Kensei caught a hint of power at Ashley's neck and noticed her necklace, and a knot of power that was carefully hidden in the pendant, eight arrows radiating from a central point.

"Can you take off your necklace?" Kensei asked.

In response, Ashley dropped to her knees and sobbed.

"I'll take that as a 'no.'"

Kensei reached down and tried to undo the clasp, with no luck. She was so tired she couldn't manage the fine dexterity. The chain seemed to be cheap and thin. Figuring that it would snap if she tugged hard enough, she grabbed the chain and gave a yank. Ashley rose up as the chain drew tight across her throat and made choking sounds while the chain refused to break. Kensei dropped the chain and snatched her hand back.

"Sorry!" Kensei gasped.

"What the hell are you doing?" Parker asked.

"I will flay the flesh from your bones," Ashley whispered as she curled in on herself.

"I'm improvising," Kensei said. "Just… Keep away from her. I'll figure this out."

Kensei reached down again, pulled up the slack of the chain and slid the edge of her sword underneath it. She pulled the blade up and back, hoping to just cut the chain. A bright light blossomed where the sword cut along the chain and then the ground fell out from underneath her.

~

First, there was darkness and the sensation of moving. And then she stood again, her body jolting from the disorientation of falling and then not. Before her sat a woman on a golden throne. She was cruel but beautiful, olive-skinned with her hair styled up and held in place with a golden comb. She wore a white, floor-length dress that left her arms bare. In some ways she felt like a spirit, but more broad in definition. She did not represent a street or a house, but instead every betrayal that had ever occurred. Every moment in which one person turned against another seemed to live within this goddess.

Kensei wore the golden *kimono* with red *hakama* again, and the lion stood at her side. She held her katana, which burned with a white light. But instead of some frigid rocky coastline, she stood in a vast hall of white marble, with white fluted columns lining each side. Between the columns hung banners of golden cloth. The smell of the sea filled the air, with hints of olive and oleander.

The woman stood, eyes wide with surprise. "What in Hades are you doing here?"

"I was going to ask the same question," Kensei said. "But I'm not going to argue with good fortune. Is it safe to assume that you're Eris, goddess of strife?"

The woman nodded.

Kensei pointed her sword at the goddess. "I'm Kensei. I believe we both know each other by reputation. I really want to know why you've had such an interest in little old me."

Eris turned and fled as the golden banners descended like snakes, one end striking out at Kensei. She dodged out of the way and sliced at them. Tatters of cloth floated through the air, the carnage of her attacks. She leapt to the side to dodge a banner that sought to wrap around her and flew farther than anticipated. Was gravity not as strong here? Did it not affect her as much? Another banner came at her and she jumped up and over with great ease. Kensei smiled. Despite the danger, this part was fun.

A roar and a blur of fur sailed past her. The lion landed on the ground with a banner in his mouth. He held it in his paws and worried it with his teeth. For a moment, she was back in the darkness with Alexis Sohda at her feet in a pool of blood, there with that lion. And then the moment passed, but not the dread and suspicion.

"I don't know who you are, Mr. Kitty," Kensei yelled. "But I'd love some answers."

The lion paused from ravaging a banner in his teeth to growl, "This is not the time."

Kensei chopped through the last of the banners and turned to face the great cat, who had also finished off his prey. "Unfortunately, I never seem to meet you in happy fun times. Where do I know you from?"

The lion began charging towards the exit that Eris had disappeared through. "Did you come here to socialize or to deal with Eris?"

Kensei followed. To her right was a cliff face, extending up at a slope with other buildings visible above. To her left, the balcony ended at a low railing, with nothing visible but a sapphire blue sea extending to the horizon. Opposite were stairs leading down the cliff face.

"Is this where Greek gods live?"

The lion sniffed at the air. "Yes. Mount Olympus. Or the mythic equivalent. The goddess went this way."

"This is a mountain…?" Kensei asked, looking about in confusion.

The lion led the way to the stairs. Kensei reached the top of the steps and saw bronze-armored soldiers running along a walkway towards her. She pegged them at about fifty. There was no sign of Eris anywhere.

"Do you have a name, lion? Or do I just get to call you Muffinbutt?"

"You just never stop," the lion said. A statement, not a question.

"You don't bring out the best in me."

"I guess I don't, do I?" The lion cocked his head at her. "You knew my name once. You will know it again."

"You suck. Muffinbutt it is. Any idea what to expect with the goons?"

"They are celestial spirits, like the *strixes*. Extensions of the gods' will. They lack souls and personalities and cannot truly die. At least not by your blade."

"Right, so no need to hold back."

"Exactly."

She ran back a few steps and then ran for the stairs, jumping down their length. She floated downward, with her clothes flapping about in the breeze. She landed feet first on the front-most soldier and knocked down several others in the process. She sliced left, sending one soldier flying over the balcony as golden liquid streamed out from his body.

Kensei waded through the troops, slicing wildly. They fell about her like wheat and their golden ichor covered her. It soaked into the silk of her kimono, leaving the cloth sticky. She paused on the far side of the carnage to catch her breath. She turned to the lion, who sat next to her and groomed his paw.

Before she could ask anything, a voice from the heavens boomed, "Titans, how dare you try to escape your prison and re-take Olympus!"

Kensei looked up to see a large, toga-wearing bearded man looking over the horizon, a writhing spear of electricity in his fist. He cocked his arm back to throw it and Kensei turned and ran back the way she came, leaping from the bottom of the steps to the top as the lightning bolt struck the cliff wall behind her and shattered stone. Another hit closer. It blasted her forward and into the marble wall above the door to Eris's hall. The impact knocked the wind out of her, so she almost didn't notice when she later hit the ground.

She felt the lion's mouth on her leg as he began to drag her into the hall. Another blast rocked the entire mountain.

"Why did he call us titans?"

"Well, either followers of other pantheons are villainous figures and fall under the generic name 'titan,' or Eris has used her ability to sow discord to turn potential divine allies against us."

Thunder and lightning exploded outside the door again, shaking the room and causing dust to rain down on them.

"I don't like either of those options. How the hell am I going to find Eris with the wrath of a god waiting for me out there?"

"If I could shrug, I would."

"What is this room anyway?" Kensei asked, thinking aloud. "Eris was trying to directly control Ashley when this all started. Could there be something special about this room? Could it be the heart of her power?"

The lion looked around. "There's power here, but there was power on the mountainside as well."

Kensei looked around, trying to focus on the spiritual aspects of the hall, which proved hard since everything here was spiritual. The throne seemed to form the heart of the place. Kensei sat in the seat and felt the power radiating all around her, lines of power extending out into infinity. Some were thick as tree trunks, others as fine as silk thread. As she thought of Ashley, she could sense her friend and thin lines of power reaching out to her.

Kensei focused on one of these lines and brought her sword down on it. It severed the line, which snapped back and struck Kensei across the face. She clutched at her face as tears and blood welled up. After several deep, shuddering breaths she felt like she could cope with the pain again. She looked over at the lion and saw her injury mirrored on his face.

Winged creatures appeared around Kensei and began to bite and claw at her. Harpies and owls were the most mundane, especially compared to the peacocks and eagles of flame that descended upon her. She slashed at them but they came in faster than she could attack. Her arms and torso burned with pain and her golden kimono hung in tatters, blood staining the fine material.

The world lurched and the light dimmed as something cut across her midsection. She fell and curled up in a ball, clutching her stomach and fending off the birds. Across from her, she saw the lion also had a cut across his belly.

"I was able to bite through a second cord," the lion said, his voice barely louder than the noise of the birds. Her attackers backed off just before a small sandaled foot kicked Kensei in the face. She wasn't able to stop the first kick, which came from Eris, but she caught the goddess's foot when she tried for a second kick. She twisted the foot and lifted, knocking Eris over and smiling at the goddess's scream of pain and rage.

Kensei lumbered over and slumped across Eris, her blood staining the goddess's white dress. She grabbed the goddess's throat with one gory hand and asked, "Why do you care about me?"

Eris spit in Kensei's face. "I was hired to do it."

"I didn't know gods went freelance." Kensei fought the urge to wipe the goddess's saliva.

"We exchange favors with one another," the goddess said.

"Jamie," the lion groaned. "More gods are coming. You must cut the last cord so we can leave this place and save Ashley."

Kensei waved him off and asked, "Who hired you?"

"Jamie!" the lion said. "I am not strong enough to cut the last. You will need to use your sword."

Through the door, she saw men and women stepping onto the balcony outside. These did not look like the faceless soldiers. Instead, she saw them as representatives of the world: the sky, the sea, the underworld, beauty, motherhood… Kensei turned to focus on the last of the cords and brought her sword down hard.

The line of connection snapped and lashed back to cut Kensei's arm. She almost dropped her weapon but managed to retain her grip. The world flipped upside down and soon all that remained was a single circle of light on white marble where she and the lion stood. As she watched, the circle began to crumble away.

She looked at the lion. Hundreds of questions came to mind, but she felt like she only had enough time to ask one. She went with the first one that came to mind.

"Is Alexis okay?"

The lion shook his head. "No, no she's not."

And then with a jolt she was back in her body, where she collapsed to the ground. Her whole body continued to hurt and she could smell a lot of blood. But the pain began to fade. She closed her eyes and relaxed into the gentle cold peace.

"She's back," Libertine announced.

"Good, then get your paws off me, Sabrina," Parker said. A moment later a hand slipped into Kensei's hand. She opened her eyes to see Parker crouched next to her. "You're going to be okay. You're a total badass."

Kensei reached over and patted the hand that held hers. She smiled, blissful at this moment. Even though someone was peeling away parts of her costume.

"If you're going to sit here, Parker," Huntsman said, "Help me with the bandages. We need to stop the bleeding if we're going to get her anywhere alive."

Kensei rolled her head in the direction of his voice and smiled at the cowled superhero. From this angle she could see up his nose. "Huntsman? You have... like a huge booger in your nose."

Parker twisted her head to look from the same angle. "Oh, man, he does."

Huntsman frowned. "This really isn't the time."

"I'll call Dr. Hao," Stardust said from somewhere nearby. "Get her ready to receive a patient."

Parker looked up. "Did you say Dr. How? Does she live in a blue box?!"

Stardust laughed. "As cool as that would be, no."

Something in the air shifted and Kensei looked over to see Karl kneeling next to her. "You did it, Miss Hattori. The spell on Karlsburg is gone."

"Hell yeah," Jamie whispered, letting her head fall back to the ground. "I did it."

CHAPTER 20 - FADE TO BLACK

Jamie and Parker walked into the school gymnasium, the loud blare of music pounding through them. It was filled with a riotous mob of dancing students under a mix of multicolored lights and strobes.

At the edge of the activity, Jamie stopped and looked at Parker. For Homecoming, Parker had bought a strapless dress with corset lacing across the back and layered petticoats that came down to her knees. Her legs were covered in fishnet stockings. She'd applied a thick layer of white makeup and then painted whimsical lines across her face. Combined with the butterfly wings strapped to her back, Parker looked like an insane Tinkerbell.

Jamie, on the other hand, had raided her mom's closet for a pants suit, burgundy with a cream colored blouse under the jacket. She was too cheap and conservative to buy a slinky dress, no matter how much Parker begged. Gloria hadn't moved back home, but had gotten an apartment within walking distance of the house. It had a spare bedroom if Jamie wanted it. Gloria had also been generous about helping Jamie pick out clothes for the dance.

"You're not chickening out, are you?" Parker asked. "You promised me two dances."

"I said 'maybe.'"

The music changed to a slower number and the crowd began to reorganize itself as couples took over the dance floor and began shuffling in time with the beat. Parker grabbed Jamie's hand and pulled her towards the dance floor.

"C'mon. If you can face down Greek gods, you can spend two minutes being soft rocked by me."

"That was hardly easy."

Parker steered Jamie into place on the dance floor and drew her close, leading them as they danced slowly together. "But you did it, Ashley seems to be fine, all your vampire owls have disappeared. And now I get to dance with my favorite badass."

After the song, they went towards the food table to review the snack options. Ashley came up to them. She wore slacks and a nice blouse. She waved awkwardly. The severing from Eris had knocked Ashley unconscious but she didn't come out of it injured like Jamie had.

"Doing okay?" Jamie asked.

Ashley nodded. "There have been some awkward questions from the police, but this is Cobalt City. Possession is a known problem. Having three former Protectorate members vouch for me helped. There wasn't any obvious connection to the blog, so that seems to still be my little secret."

"It's your little secret you're getting rid of, right?" Parker asked.

"It's already gone. I also wrote a virus to hunt down archived copies on the Web and destroy them. *Tabula rasa.*"

"Aces," Parker said.

Jamie spotted Sabrina stalking through the gym with her tuxedo-clad date. Jamie half recognized him as being part of the football team. He looked like a gorilla in a suit with his broad shoulders and thick arms. He followed one step behind Sabrina like a trained dog. Sabrina wore a crimson backless floor-length dress with a choker neck. Jamie and Sabrina made eye contact and gave each other a slight nod of acknowledgement. Sabrina had her game face on, apparently unwilling to acknowledge Jamie any more than that.

"Earth to Jamie," Parker said.

Jamie snapped her head back. "Huh?"

"We need to get you a new costume."

"What?"

"You're buds with A-list masks. You need to look like you belong."

"What's wrong with my costume?"

"You look like a minion, not a superhero."

Jamie pinched Parker's arm. "Can we not talk about this here?"

"Fine, but both Sabrina and I agree: Your eyes are a dead giveaway in your mask. Anyone who knows you can recognize you in that getup."

"So, wait… you and Sabrina are conspiring against me?"

Parker sneered. "No, we just had time to talk while you were in your staring contest with Ashley. You really need to up your game and conceal your identity better if you're going to do this."

"What is so weird about my eyes?" Jamie asked. "This makes three people who have said this."

"They're not weird," Parker said. "Just beautiful and… distinctive."

Jamie squirmed at the attention. "If you say so."

"I do," Parker said. "I spend a lot of time looking at and thinking about your eyes."

The music changed again and Parker perked up. "I love this song! We have to go dance."

"But—"

Parker grabbed Jamie's hand. "Two dances. I remember a promise even if you deny it."

Jamie laughed as she was dragged back to the dance floor and waved to Ashley. Life was good, and she could get used to this.

~

Eris's slaves dragged her trireme up onto the rocky coastline as a cold rain fell. Farther inland, the rocks gave way to tall, green grass with a well-worn trail that led up to a sod-covered longhouse.

The goddess stood on deck, shivering under her thick shawl. She hated this place, but the god she sought was not responding to her summons. And she would not be denied a chance to speak her mind to this fool, even if it meant sailing through the Coil to this blighted land.

With her slaves' aid, she descended onto the coastline and walked up the trail to the longhouse. Her honor guard hurried to catch up. Halfway up the trail, he emerged from his house, the red of his overtunic almost as bright as his hair.

He leaned against the doorway and smiled. "Sweet lady of strife, what brings you to this harsh corner of the world?"

"You know very well what brings me, you honey-tongued bastard."

He laughed, but feigned innocence. Placing a hand on his chest, he said, "Me? You assume a lot of me. I have, at times, been a woman, but it's never given me insight into the workings of their minds."

"The half-breed you sent me after brought war to Olympus and severed my connection to my avatar." The rain soaked through her dress but her anger kept her warm.

"You should have been more careful," the man said. "When one plays with fire, one is known to get burned."

"You set me up to fail, didn't you?" Eris asked. "You knew this could happen, didn't you?"

"That's a strong accusation."

"Don't play coy with me, you two-faced toad. How could you use me so ill? I should think you would have more respect for a kindred spirit."

The man laughed and shook his head. "If we are kindred spirits, and I am a two-faced toad, what does that make you?" He raised a hand before she could respond and stood up straight. "Please, if there is anyone in your family that I share a bond to it is more likely to be Hermes, or poor bound Prometheus, than some petulant troublemaker who starts wars because she doesn't get a wedding invitation. Causing two rocks to bang together is the action of a toddler, not a masterful liar who plays a long game."

"So you admit that you set me up to fail?" Eris asked. "Is this what I get for trusting Loki?"

"If the simple phrase 'trusting Loki' does not sound absurd," Loki said, "then I think you have a lot more to learn. Did I set you up to fail? No. Even the lowest pawn can become a queen. But sometimes you have to sacrifice a piece. The very fact that you did something for me should make the fact that I 'used' you obvious. But you failed on your own merits, and not through any artifice of mine."

Eris glared at the Norse god. "Do not think I am done with you. Or your target. I am not one to be played with or betrayed."

Loki shrugged. "I understand, though I encourage you to arrange something a bit more dangerous than a beauty contest. Not that it would have much effect. The very fact that Thor was able to disguise himself as *our* goddess of beauty should really say something about our standards. I doubt there will be much squabbling among the Aesir about who 'the fairest' is."

Eris spun on her heel and stalked back to her ship.

Loki waved farewell and ducked into the longhouse, out of the rain.

ABOUT THE AUTHOR

Jeremy Zimmerman is a teller of tales who dislikes cute euphemisms for writing like "teller of tales." His fiction has most recently appeared in 10Flash Quarterly, Arcane and anthologies from Timid Pirate Publishing. He is also the editor for Mad Scientist Journal. He lives in Seattle with five cats and his lovely wife (and fellow author) Dawn Vogel. To learn more about Jeremy, visit his site at www.bolthy.com.

ABOUT THE ILLUSTRATOR

Based in Seattle, Katie Nyborg is a writer, illustrator, and fairy tale collector. She's composed primarily of ghosts, peppermint patties, and an overactive imagination. More of her work and worlds can be found at katiedoesartthings.tumblr.com.

www.ingramcontent.com/pod-product-compliance
Lightning Source LLC
Chambersburg PA
CBHW060422130626
46555CB00005B/2173